CLOSER THAN

ENEMIES

By

KAREN MARIE COLEMAN

Karen Coleman

ISBN-10 1732831424

ISBN-13 978-1732831421

Kaldonya Brunson
PUBLISHING

authorkarencoleman@yahoo.com

Visit our official Website at: www.karencoleman.org

Table of Contents

Chapter One

On her way to the restaurant to meet her friend Kimberly for their lunch date, Peyton fumbled through her purse for her ringing cell phone. Her friend called to inform her that she was running a few minutes late. She was only a few minutes away from the restaurant. After ending her call, she turned the volume up on her radio and proceeded to the restaurant. Peyton was in a great mood because several projects that she'd been working on were going great, and she was finally getting a chance to settle back into her normal routine. She was happy to be meeting her friend for lunch. Because of their busy schedules, they hadn't had a chance to talk much in the past couple of weeks. They try to make regular lunch dates at least twice a month. On this day, they are trying out a fairly new restaurant. This eatery was not on the usual lists of places that they would normally dine, especially for women of their means, but a friend highly recommended it. It was off the beaten path, located in the urban part of Memphis, a part of town that was somewhat undesirable due to the high crime rate.

Peyton pulled into the restaurant's parking lot. The place was packed with customers. She scanned the lot, looking for an available parking space. She was lucky enough to catch someone leaving.

Walking inside, she was reminded of her many visits to the heart of New Orleans. The aroma of authentic Creole and Cajun-style cuisine wafted across her nose, giving off a heavenly scent that piqued her interest. The owners were from New Orleans, Louisiana. She was told that they served some of the best food around. The food smelled great, and she was hungry. She skipped breakfast to make room for the calories she knew she'd consume for lunch. She looked around for the wait staff.

The place was standing room only, and there was hardly an available table anywhere in the restaurant. After waiting a few minutes, a young man walked to where she was standing. "Hello, ma'am. Welcome to The Ultimate Gras. How many are in your party?"

"Two. My friend is on the way. She should be here in about ten minutes," said Peyton. She was given a table and two menus. Once she was seated, she ordered an iced tea. Afterward, she took a little time to look around the restaurant. Although not very upscale, the place looked okay. It was clean and neat. She noticed the tablecloths were gold, green, and purple. There were images of saxophones, masks, and beads on the walls. Large photographic images of famed jazz musicians donned the walls. The place looked like an extension of a Mardi Gras celebration. Peyton relaxed in her seat. Since her friend took a little longer than usual, she checked her messages.

After a few minutes, Kimberly rushed in.

"Hey, girl!" Kimberly breathed out heavily as she set her things down in her booth seat. Her long, silky black hair, with hints of blonde highlights, was tangled all over her face because of the wind. She brushed her hair from her face with perfectly manicured nails. She pulled her scarf away from her neck and unbuttoned her jacket to the ivory-colored designer pantsuit she was wearing, and then she wriggled her six-foot frame into her seat.

"I'm sorry I'm late," she said. She proceeded to tell her friend about her busy morning.

"I had a meeting that ran a little over with pushy clients. I had to do what it took to pacify them. What I really wanted was to wring their freaking necks with their indecisive asses. They wore me out with all that damn negotiating. I'm exhausted!"

"Well sweetie, that's why you make the big bucks. You're the reason that law firm is doing so well, and that's why they courted you so hard to become a partner. You're their master negotiator. You've made millions for that firm. You've accomplished all of that amidst, what do you call it? *The Good-ole-Boys Network....* You're the first black woman to break through the glass ceiling at that firm. You're one of their best attorneys."

"Yes, but sometimes I feel as if they don't appreciate me. I mean, is it too much to ask for a little more appreciation for all my hard work? The more I accomplish, the more work they heap on my back, and what for? A measly ass, congratulations. I mean, don't get me wrong, the money is great, but damn. No other partner, and I mean no one, has accomplished what I have, yet they throw parties, give perks, and all that other shit to them. Half of the major clients at the firm are the ones I brought in myself. I was thinking of possibly branching off and doing my own thing. I will, just as soon as the timing is right, and I'm taking all of my clients with me."

Their waitress said, "Hello, I'm Nikki; I'm your server today; let me know when you're ready to order." Kimberly looked across the table at Peyton and said,

"I'm thirsty; I need a cold drink of something. What are you drinking?"

"Iced tea," Peyton said, shaking her glass. Kimberly ordered an iced tea as well.

"I want vodka on the rocks but still have clients to see." Kimberly relaxed for a moment and settled in her seat. She studied Peyton for a second.

"Wow, girl, you look great today! What have you done differently? Peyton had a new stylist who was trying a bolder, sexier look for her. She's more of the conservative type. She often wore clothing that downplayed her figure and wore minimal makeup, if she wore any at all. So now that she has on bolder colors and is wearing makeup, Kimberly notices the new look. Peyton worked out three times a week and she's an avid runner. She's five feet tall and weighs just under a hundred-twenty pounds. Although she's petite, her body is toned. She's a natural beauty, but she's a plain Jane. She has a smooth, honey-colored complexion with beautiful light brown eyes. Her shoulder length is a natural light brown.

"I have a new stylist," Peyton tells her.

"I like what she's done for you. You really ought to keep her because you're looking fabulous."

"Thank you. Initially, I thought I looked ridiculous, but my hubby loved the new look so much that I decided to keep it."

"It's working for you." Kimberly began looking around the restaurant. With a slight frown on her face, she asked,

"Girl, what made you choose *this* place?"

"Carol from the gym recommended it. I was curious, so here we are!"

"The food here must be great because I've never known you to visit this side of town for anything." Peyton, looking around the place, replied,

"You know, sometimes the best food is not always in five-star restaurants but in smaller places like this. There's nothing wrong with trying something a little different for a change, is there? But if we enjoy the food here, we will have to send for it instead of coming down here by ourselves. We don't want to get mugged," Peyton said jokingly.

"I feel bad for the person who would dare try. You know that I won't sit still long enough to allow that."

Kimberly is beautiful, but she's tough. She can be a classy lady one minute and kick ass the next. In her own words, *"I don't take shit from anyone!"* She had proven herself to be quite tough in high school when a group of jealous girls picked a fight with her. She beat them hands down. If a guy would get a little aggressive with her for spurning his advances, she'd promptly get him in check. When she was younger, her father enrolled her in martial arts and self-defense classes. That, along with her strong, dominant nature, makes for a real ballbuster type of lady.

"What have you been up to since I last saw you?" Kimberly asked.

"I've been busy at the ministry. As you may know, our girls are competing in the beauty pageant this year, so we are getting ready for that. Also, the food drive for the city's needy has really picked up. Gil and I have increased our monetary gift this year because there seems to be a bigger need. The economy has left a lot of folks in need. Several other companies have matched our donations, so we are preparing the food for delivery to the local food banks. Mayor Wendell James got into it this year, and now he wants to throw a gala honoring Gil, me, and others who gave. You know we have the big election coming up this year, so he will probably go all out. From what I'm hearing, it will be a major event. We've been preparing for that."

"Oh, I'm glad you mentioned it," Kimberly said while getting her billfold. "I intended to give you my check at our last luncheon. You know the busy schedule I keep. I don't get to the church as often as I should." She began to write a check for the food drive. "Now you, on the other hand, spend way too much time at the ministry. You can do anything you want to. Why not hire somebody else to do that or, at the very least, assist you."

Kimberly ripped the check from her checkbook. "I don't mind giving to the cause, but I don't have time for all that volunteering. Besides, with the money you have, I would be traveling instead of being stuck in some church, especially since you've given up your career. I still don't understand why." Peyton smiled and said,

"I don't mind Kimberly. I enjoy it, and I feel that it's where I belong. It's what I love. Volunteering is my passion."

"I have passion, too," Kimberly replied, "That's why I donate cash."

"There's nothing wrong with that," Peyton said with a smile. "As long as you do what's in your heart to do, you're doing your part. I know you have compassion for others and the things of God. You're a good girl; you just have a bad girl streak that rears her pretty little head occasionally. You're kind, thoughtful, and generous. You're always considerate of others, and you're a hard worker. So what, if you like to party a lot, that's okay with me. That's just you being you. I love you just the way you are. I wouldn't trade you for anything."

Kimberly has a strong personality. She comes off as assertive, aggressive, and very harsh. Peyton feels that her friend is often misunderstood. She chooses to see the good in everyone, even in her best friend. Peyton is a sweet, mild-mannered person. Her smile is warm, and her words are always comforting. She's soft-spoken and easy to get along with. She's a joy to be around.

Kimberly produced a grateful smile.

"You see, Peyton, that's why I love you. You never judge me or look down your nose at me. You're always kind to me, and you always have my back."

"You're my girl; you know I got you," said Peyton.

"What did I do to deserve you as a friend? You're so understanding and loving toward me. I mean, I love God and all, and I attend church sometimes. People often judge me because I do my own thing. I can't stand some of these judgmental, holy-roller, bible-beating folks. They're all up in my business, looking down their nose at me while sitting on their broke assed morals. Some of them make me so mad," Kimberly said, looking disgusted.

"I understand what you mean," Peyton said, picking up her menu, "They shouldn't act that way towards others, but that's how some people are. When they behave that way, they're not walking in love. They tend to lose the person they're supposedly trying to help because they lack understanding of the person. When they're critical or judgmental, their message gets lost in their criticism. They give people a bad taste in their mouths for the church and the things of God. Some of them believe that God doesn't want them to enjoy their lives, so they put themselves on this strict religious path that they're unhappy with. When they see anyone else attempting to enjoy their lives, they become critical of that person, sometimes even angry. Perhaps they're only angry because maybe secretly, they would like to do their own thing."

"Well, maybe they need to go and get laid and ask for forgiveness later. If they keep getting into my business, then I will be at the altar praying for forgiveness for snatching one of them up. They both laugh. "Girl, you're crazy," Peyton said while shaking her head and looking at the menu.

Kimberly blurted out, "I'm hungry as hell. Where's our waitress?"

"I'm hungry too. I'll get her attention. What are you ordering?"

"I have a busy afternoon. I don't want to feel sluggish, so I need to eat lightly. What about you?"

"As you can see by this menu, there's hardly anything light on it. I came here to indulge a little, so I'll have something full of fat and calories."

"You can afford to eat that way as thin as you are," said Kimberly. They got their waitress and ordered while continuing to update each other on their lives.

"How are things going with you and Gil?"

"We're great," Peyton replied with a girlish delight. After many years of marriage, Peyton is still in love with her husband, Gilbert Wilkes.

Gil is her dream guy. He's an award-winning, board-certified plastic surgeon in the state of Tennessee, with more high-profile clients than anyone in the South. Among his clientele are Hollywood celebrities and the wealthiest elite who travel from all over the world to have him perform their surgeries. He's considered one of the best surgeons in his field. He lectures at medical schools all over the country. He owns a four-story, state-of-the-art surgery center, in the heart of the city. He owns real estate around the globe. He also owns many properties in the Memphis area, mainly luxury condos. He has a portfolio that's worth millions.

Gil comes from a good family. His mother was a stay-at-home mom, and his father is a primary care physician with two family practice clinics that he still operates. Gil studied a lot and rarely dated coming up. He didn't hang out much, choosing rather to stay focused on his studies. Peyton was his second girlfriend. They met when they were in their early twenties. They were friends for close to six months before they decided to date. They were married two years later. After Peyton passed the bar, they stopped renting and purchased their first home. Once he finished his residency at Brookhaven Medical, he opened his private practice, which is thriving wonderfully. Peyton, eating her lunch, said,

"Gil is busy at the clinic. He has a couple of surgeries today. He's going to call me when he's done."

Kimberly, wanting her views to be known, said,

"Girl, I still don't see how you handle him looking at all those beautiful women all day, playing with their breasts." Kimberly never missed an opportunity to aim cheap shots at Gil. Peyton couldn't seem to figure out why she seemed to dislike him so much. Peyton brushed it off because she knew Kimberly meant nothing by it. Kimberly has always been critical of men.

"You have a sick mind." Peyton laughed. "It's a part of his job."

"Yeah, but has it ever crossed your mind that he'd be tempted to just pop one of those big ole breasts in his mouth?"

"No," Peyton said while slapping at Kimberly, "But I can see that it's crossed your mind. He's not like that; besides, Gil knows what he has at home. He knows I'm his good thing."

"Yeah, but how does he handle all that temptation?" Kimberly scoffed.

"Gil is a godly man, and he's wise. He loves me, and what we have is solid. We've built a wonderful life together, and he's not willing to do anything to destroy that." Looking at Peyton unconvinced, Kimberly said, "He's fine and rich; you had better watch him because somebody may want to try him. I have to tell you that all the time. He's still a man. Name me one man who hasn't or doesn't cheat on his woman. You know all men cheat." Peyton smiled and sipped her iced tea, "Well, I'm not worried about that. But since we're talking about men, when are you going to settle down and get *yourself* a man? You haven't had a date in quite some time now." Kimberly looking disgusted,

"Girl, please... You know I'm not even trying to go there. Men are useless. I have no time for their foolishness. They're indecisive, selfish, childish, and untrustworthy. What can a man offer me? My net worth is four-point-five million dollars and counting. I have everything that I want. The way I see it, men are only good for sex, and some of them aren't even good at that. I'm just not that interested. They bore me. They have no real conversation; you've heard my horror stories. I can feel my skin melting from my face when listening to them talk. Even guys who are supposedly intellectuals are boring, with no real conversation. Men show little interest in the things that matter to a woman. They're so stuck on themselves and their wants nowadays.

They're not like the men in the old days who used to love and cherish their women like our fathers or our grandfathers; you know, they used to take care of a lady back then. That's when men were men, and they would look out for a woman's every need."

"You're always saying men are bad. Not all men are bad. You've got to keep looking; you'll find the right guy for you," Peyton said, looking hopeful for her friend.

"Look at me, girl. I'm almost forty, and I haven't found one yet; I'm exhausted. I gave up on that trip a long time ago. So, I focus on me and my work." Peyton shook her head.

"It's not over for you. You can't give up. Your work won't soothe those lonely nights. What *do* you do when you get lonely?" Kimberly downplayed the conversation, not wanting to discuss her love life or lack thereof.

"I just throw a slumber party with a few of the girls. I'm content. I don't need a man. Trust me. I *was* thinking about getting a dog, though. If you're going to have a dog, it may as well be a real one." Peyton laughed uncontrollably.

"Now, you know you're crazy."

"I'm for real, girl," Kimberly said while leaning back in her seat, looking as though she'd just discovered the meaning of life.

"Well, I guess you've thought of everything?" They continued their conversation. The two always lose track of time when they're together, and they regret having to part ways. The time had come for them to end their lunch date, . Kimberly began gathering her things.

"Well, I'm going to see you next week; call me later, okay." Kimberly hugged Peyton,

"Love you, girl."

"Bye." Kimberly left.

Peyton texted her husband, got her things, and left the restaurant. Initially, she had planned on stopping by her church, but she decided to stop by her father's law firm, Brockington and Associates. Peyton worked as a full-time attorney soon after obtaining her law degree. She worked at Brockington and Associates until she decided to leave a year and a half ago. She was a great attorney, but it wasn't what she saw herself doing for the rest of her life. It simply wasn't in her heart. Her father, on the other hand, ate, slept, and breathed law. He wanted his daughter to follow in his footsteps, so he groomed her in the field. She entered into law because of her father. If she'd chosen to pursue her passion, she would've become an educator. She enjoyed children and she dreamt of becoming a teacher, but due to the pressure from her father, she went into law. Since she was no longer practicing law; she had a lot of extra time on her hands to do as she pleased.

She enjoyed volunteering, working out, gardening, and cooking. She also enjoyed caring for her husband and spending quality time with him. The Wilke's are philanthropists, often making hefty financial contributions for scholarships, homeless ministries, and many other humanitarian causes. They have plenty, and they love sharing what they have. Peyton is great at fundraising. Along with mentoring the youth, this was a major part of what she did when volunteering at the church.

She pulled up at the three-thousand-square-foot building in the downtown district. She noticed her dad's SUV in the parking lot. She parked in her reserved parking spot that still bore her name and went inside. Mrs. Margaret Wilson, the office manager, greeted her with a warm welcome. The elderly lady looked as if she'd just left the beauty salon. Her silver mane was tightly curled into a neatly cut bob. Her edges were slicked down to the sides of her deep brown skin. Peyton could smell a hint of the salon products that had been used on her hair. The lady often used her lunch break to get her hair curled, especially if she had an event to attend the same evening. Margaret has been an office manager with the law firm since it opened thirty-plus years ago. She's a kind, warm-hearted lady. She's still married to her husband of forty-two years. She refused to retire because, as she puts it, "Who else is going to run this place?" Mrs. Wilson has run the firm's day-to-day operations for years. As business began to grow and modern technology came into play, her job duties changed from running the place to basically being a receptionist. She knows everything that goes on at the firm, and despite her age, she's pretty sharp. Everyone loves and respects her, and she's a motherly presence in the office. She is practically a member of the Brockington family.

"Hello, Mrs. Wilson! How are you?"

"Child, I'm doing alright today. If I can get this old arthritis in my knee to calm down, I'd be doing much better. Other than that, I'm fine. I took naproxen for pain. I have a hot date with my husband tonight. It's his birthday. But you don't want to hear about us old folks. How have you been? I haven't seen you around in a while. Is everything okay?"

"Yes, everything's fine. I just stopped by to say hi to Dad. Is he busy?"

"No, he's not. He just got out of a meeting, and now he's back there getting ready to eat a late lunch."

"You mean he hasn't eaten all day?"

"No, he hasn't. Your mom cooked all that food for him, but he's been too busy to eat it."

"Mom's going to kill him." Peyton hurried back to her dad's office.

On her way, she passed her old office and noticed it was still intact. It looked as though she still worked there. She paused for a moment and drew in a deep breath. She let out a relieving sigh, convinced that leaving was the best choice she could've made. She quickly walked into her father's office. She lightly tapped his door and made her way inside. He stood near the library shelf, sifting through law books for a specific case he was working on.

'Hi, Dad!" she said with all the excitement of a daddy's girl. He's always delighted to see her. When he noticed it was her, the hefty, five-foot-nine, solid-built man turned into mush seeing his daughter. She hugged him.

"Hey, there, baby girl. How are you doing?"

"I would be doing great if you'd take better care of yourself," she said, loosening her embrace.

"You know you need to eat. You're already borderline diabetic, and you have high blood pressure; you can't be skipping meals."

"I haven't skipped any meals. I'm about to eat right now."

"Dad, you're eating a late lunch. It's going on at two o'clock. What would Mom say if she knew?"

"You two worry too much about me. I'll be alright." As long as I have two of the most beautiful girls in the world in my life, I'm not going anywhere."

"Well, you'd better not," Peyton said. "Just take better care of yourself for me." Peyton's father sat down on the edge of his desk. She took a seat.

"So, what brings you by today?"

"I was on my way to the church when I decided to stop by to check on you."

"When you go by the church, tell Pastor Hawkins that I'll see him at the board meeting on Thursday evening."

"Yes, sir, deacon Brockington," she said to her father. "I'll tell him as soon as I see him. So, Daddy, what case are you working on now?"

"I'm still working that wrongful death Hemingway lawsuit. We're suing on behalf of the families involved. We have to get the ball rolling on this one. The statutes of limitations are running out. Two employees were killed on the job during an accident due to faulty machinery. The company is clearly negligent, but its lawyers have held the case up with so much red tape by blaming the workers and trying to prove that they were negligent. They've bullied their entire workforce, and everyone who witnessed the incident is afraid to come forward out of fear of losing their jobs. They've even relocated some of their workers to other plants. They're trying to buy time enough for the statute of limitations to run out." He tells her more about the case.

"That isn't right. Why are they doing that?" she asked after hearing what her father had to say about the case.

"Clearly, they're at fault here. They are trying to cover their behinds by shaking up the workforce and intimating witnesses. Daddy, you can't let them get away with that."

"I plan to do all I can to get justice for their loved ones," he said as he got a cigar and lit it. "Look at you, baby girl; you're all fired up like you want to do something about it!"

"Oh no, Daddy, I'm just saying. So, who do you have working on the case with you?"

"I have Stanley and Gabe; they're the best around here."

"Well, what about Kimberly? You know that she's very good and the top attorney at her firm."

"Yeah, she is," her father said, puffing on his cigar. "She's doing pretty good for herself. I see she's finally made partner. She's over there making all that money for those white folks. She should've stayed here. I still miss our old team. I'm happy for her, though. I've been following her progress her entire career, but I happen to know someone who's much better than she is."

"Oh really," Peyton said, eager to know who this attorney could be.

"Who, Dad?"

"You, baby girl," he said proudly. "You're a far better attorney than Kimberly."

"Oh, you're biased."

"No, I mean it. You were trained by the best. I taught you both well. Have you considered coming back, dear? You know your office is still waiting on you."

"Now, Daddy, you know that I've moved on to other things."

"I understand, but why don't you return just for this case we're working on now? I can use all the hands I can get."

"No, Dad," Peyton said. "I can't. I'm too busy."

"Busy doing what, baby?"

"Oh, Dad," she said, brushing him off.

"If you change your mind, you know where to find me."

"Yes, I do," she said, "right here in this office as usual. I have to leave, but I'll call you and Mom later." Peyton got up from her seat and walked over to her father, who was still sitting at the edge of his desk.

"I love you, Dad," she said, hugging him. I'll see you later."

"Bye, baby girl; think about what I said, okay."

"Daddy, you never give up, *do* you?"

Mr. Brockington got up, walked Peyton to the door, and entered the reception area. Peyton turned to her father and said,

"Dad, please eat something!"

"I will, so you can stop worrying." She left. She got in her car, but she didn't leave right away. She stared at her name on her personal parking space, and she gripped her steering wheel. She thought about the early days when she worked there and the great memories. She thought of her first day, her father's pride, and how excited he was to have her working there. He threw her a welcome reception. She remembered when she won her first case, and her father began trusting her with the big cases. She didn't miss the work all that much; actually, she did not miss that part at all. She missed the wonderful times she shared while working closely with her father. She quickly gathered her thoughts. She started her car and left.

She didn't go to the church as she had planned. Instead, she decided to cook a nice meal for her husband. She wanted to spend a romantic evening with him. Although they do employ a personal chef, she still does most of the cooking at home, especially for her husband. She used their personal chef for major parties. Even then, she was supervising and helping to prepare meals, especially those secret recipes that had been passed down through her family for generations. She drove to the market. She wanted fresh lamb chops not frozen. She got the chops she needed and some fresh vegetables. She also purchased fresh strawberries for a strawberry cheesecake that Gil loved. She hurried home to get things prepared for dinner. She called Gil to tell him they would be dining at home.

Chapter Two

The Hospital Visit

Peyton was awakened by her cell phone ringing. Still sleepy, she stumbled over her shoes, trying to find her purse. She noticed the clock read five o'clock a.m. She and Gil had been up most of the night enjoying each other. She started to let the call go to her voicemail, but since it was early, she thought she had better answer it.

"Hello"

"Peyton," the voice on the other end cried out softly but was a bit disturbed.

"Mom, what's going on? Why are you crying?"

"It's your father."

"What about Dad?" she asked. Gil, overhearing the conversation, quickly sat up in bed.

"When I woke, I looked at him, but he didn't look well. He gripped his chest and then he fell to the floor. I tried to talk to him, but he didn't respond. I don't know what's going on. The med flight is here. They're taking him to the emergency room. Please get to Brookhaven Medical right now. Hurry! I am riding with him in the helicopter."

"Okay, Mom," Peyton said, motioning for Gil to get his clothes on.

"We're on our way." Peyton ended the call and quickly got dressed.

"What's going on baby?" Gil asked.

"Dad's being rushed to the hospital by med flight; they're taking him to Brookhaven Medical."

Gil got out of bed and got dressed. He pressed the intercom,

"Mr. Banks, bring the car around front and hurry."

"Okay Mr. Wilkes," the man's voice on the other end replied. They both hurried to the car.

"I'll drive myself," Gil said to the driver.

"We're in a hurry." Gil hopped in the driver's seat, and they left for the hospital. When they arrived, they met Peyton's mother in the emergency room. She sat with her arms folded, waiting for word from her husband. Peyton rushed to her side.

"What's wrong with dad?"

"I don't know yet. They've taken him back to the exam room. I've already contacted his doctor." Mrs. Brockington said.

"When will we know something, Mom?"

"I'm not sure?" Peyton ran to the nurse's station and asked one of the nurses what was going on with her father. Gil was already in the back. He knew most of the emergency room doctors on call.

"Our staff is doing everything they can to make sure that Mr. Brockington is getting the best care," the nurse said trying to reassure Peyton.

"What's wrong with him?" she asked.

"Someone will be out shortly to tell you what's happening." While the nurse was speaking, Gil came out of the back. Peyton and Mrs. Brockington went to him. "What's happening, Gil?" Peyton asked.

"Pop has suffered a heart attack. He's in the coronary care unit. They're helping him now. Mr. Arnold has arrived, and he's with him. He's okay. He's alert and resting comfortably. They had to get him stabilized."

"When can we see him?" Mrs. Brockington asked.

"You can go back right now." Peyton and her mom followed Gil to the C.C.U. Mr. Brockington was lying on the gurney hooked up to an EKG machine with an oxygen mask on and an IV in his arm. He was happy to see his family. Peyton rushed to her father's side.

"Well, there are my favorite girls." Mr. Brockington said, trying to be in good spirits. He didn't want them worrying about him. Mrs. Brockington kissed him.

"Are you okay?" she asked while taking his hand.

"I'm fine. I just had a little problem with my heart."

"A little!" Peyton said as she stepped back and looked at her father with a stern facial expression.

"You had a heart attack, Daddy! I would say that that's a pretty big deal. I told you to take better care of yourself." While Peyton was talking to her father, his doctor entered the room. Dr. Arnold Moore was a close friend of the Brockington family. They attend the same church. He, Gil, and Mr. Brockington play golf together whenever time permits.

"Hey there Gil, how's it going?" Dr. Moore asked as he shook Gil's hand. "I haven't had a chance to talk to you since you whipped me in that golf game. What was it? About three months ago?"

"Yes, it's been a minute. But you could've easily whipped me. I wasn't up to my full swing, if you know what I mean."

"Yeah, I've got to work on my game." Concerned for her father, Peyton looked at Gil and the doctor in disgust, "If you two are finished!"

"Hello Peyton," Dr. Moore said hugging her.

"Hello Vanessa," he said to Mrs. Brockington.

"Arnold, what's going on with Henry?

"He had a mild heart attack. We gave him nitroglycerin, heparin, and a little aspirin. We got him all fixed up, but I must keep him here for a couple of days. I want to run some tests on his heart, and I want to watch his blood pressure. He will be okay, but he needs to take it easy."

"When will I be able to go back to work, Arnie?" The doctor looked at his chart and then at Mr. Brockington.

"I don't want you to think about work right now, Henry. You've had a close call and you should take your health seriously. You should think about taking a little time off to rest and get better. You shouldn't be doing anything stressful, and you definitely shouldn't be thinking about work right now."

"I have this big case that I'm working on. What am I going to do? I'm right in the middle of this thing; the boys can't do it alone. They may need me there." Peyton interrupted him.

"Dad, I'm sure that Stanley and Gabe can handle everything. They've always done a great job for you, even when you're not there."

"Yeah, but I'm still involved in everything they do." I'm never too far away from all the action."

"That's part of your problem now—too much action and not enough rest. The law firm will run smoothly with or without you. You hired well-capable attorneys. They're loyal and committed. You should rest like the doctor said and leave everything up to *us*."

Peyton said, *us* without thinking about it. She began thinking about that statement. She knew she would have to return to the firm, at least for now. She loved her father tremendously and couldn't stand the thought of anything happening to him. She also knew that her father was a little stubborn, and he really didn't trust anybody wholeheartedly with his business, a business he'd built from the ground up. A business that's not only his passion but his very life. He would rather die than see his life's dream destroyed. The only person he ever trusted was Peyton. She was the only one who ran his firm, and she showed the kind of passion that he had for his clients. She knew the law very well. He shared everything that he knew with her. He did this purposely because he wanted her to keep the firm going when he retired.

Mrs. Brockington broke her train of thought with a sigh.

"Well, we know what you'll be doing, Mr. Workaholic. You'll be resting and getting better—enough talk about the firm. Arnie, I'll be staying here with him. When will his room be ready?"

"I'll have the nurse handle all that for you." Dr. Moore slapped Mr. Brockington on the leg,

"Henry, take care of yourself, and I'll see you later this evening." Mr. Brockington exhaled and said, "I guess I have no choice in the matter." Dr. Moore left. Everyone was relieved that he was going to be okay. Gil walked over to the bed,

"Pop, you gave us quite a scare there. Arnie is right; you do need to take better care of yourself. You've been working so hard lately."

"Yes, he has," Mrs. Brockington said. He works all day and most nights. He brings his work home with him and often falls asleep while working in his office. I have to go in and make him come to bed most nights."

"Well, all that's going to change. We want you to get well. We need you, daddy."

"We sure do pop," Gil said. Gil took Peyton's hand.

"Honey, I'm going to go and grab some breakfast. Would you like for me to get something for you?"

"I'm coming with you." Peyton wanted to discuss the possibility of her temporarily returning to the firm.

"Mom, can we bring you something back?" Peyton asked.

"No, I'm okay; I don't feel like eating yet."

"Alright, I'll be back shortly." Peyton kissed her dad, and they left.

Peyton called home to inform the cook to have breakfast ready. After she ended the call, she and Gil discussed her going back to work.

"Are you sure you want to do that, honey? Especially since you were so adamant about not going back."

"I have no choice. I feel that I need to do this. You know how Dad is about the firm. He'll return to work before he's supposed to, and that's not what he needs right now. It won't be permanent. I can go back now and help with this lawsuit. Anything else, I'm sure the guys can handle."

"Peyton honey, they're already in the middle of this case. Are you sure you'll be able to catch up this late in the game?"

"I believe I'll be alright. I'll get with Dad, and I'll call a meeting with the guys, and we'll go from there."

"Okay," Gil said. "You know what you want to do. It seems like you already have your mind made up. I'll support you no matter what you choose." Peyton smiled and kissed him on the cheek.

"I know you will baby." Peyton changed the subject.

"So baby, what time do you think you'll be finished with work today?"

"I should be home no later than six this evening. I have two surgeries, and the rest are follow-ups. I'll call throughout the day to check on Pop," Gil said. They made it home. Gil ate his breakfast, showered, and left for the clinic. Peyton made a few phone calls. She called the firm to let Mrs. Wilson know about her father. She scheduled a meeting with the other attorneys. Mr. Brockington has several attorneys who work at the firm. His firm handles business litigation and personal injury cases, wrongful death, and various other forms of law.

Peyton made a few more calls. She canceled most of her appointments, showered, and took a quick nap. As soon as she dozed off, her cell phone rang. It was Kimberly. During all the commotion, she had forgotten to call her. Peyton told her about her father.

"I'm so sorry, girl! Is he alright?"

"He's doing much better now; they're keeping him for a couple of days for observation. He should be home soon." Peyton sat up in bed.

"Mom is still there with him. You know it'll take a crowbar to get her to leave his side." Peyton looked at the clock; it was twelve-fifteen She got out of bed.

"Girl, I gotta go; I'll call you later." Peyton ended the call.

She prepared chicken salad sandwiches, fresh fruit, and bottled water and left for the hospital. When she got to her father's room, she noticed that her mother was still by his side. She had slipped her small frame into bed with her father and was lying in his arms. Her mother was the strength of the family. She's a devoted wife who made time for Peyton and her father. Her family came first, and she never allowed anyone or anything to interfere with her taking care of them.

"Peyton, you made it back?"

"Hey, Mom. How's Dad?" They whispered because he was sleeping.

"He's doing much better."

"I prepared a little food." Peyton set the food on a small dresser in the room. Her mom went over to see what was in the bags; she got a sandwich and a bottle of water.

"Mom, I think you need to go home and get a shower and a nap. Let me take care of Dad for a little while. He's doing much better now, and you could use the rest."

"Now child," she said with one hand on her hip, "You know I'm not about to be lying around the house while your father is laid up in this hospital bed. I'll go and get a shower and get some things for him to make his stay here a little more tolerable, but I'll be staying here with him until all of this is over.

"Okay Mom," Peyton said. She knew there was no use in arguing with her. Mrs. Brockington ate and went home to shower while Peyton watched her father. She read a book while her dad rested.

Chapter Three

BACK TO WORK

Mr. Brockington was released from the hospital. His doctor assigned a private nurse for him for the next couple of weeks. Dr. Moore felt it best if he were back in his own environment. This would help him to recover faster. Mr. Brockington was headstrong and outgoing. He thrived on mixing and mingling with people. He's not the kind of man that can be cooped up for long periods stressed him more than his illness, so although Dr. Moore still had some concerns, he decided that his being released with a private nurse would be better for him. The family agreed. In the meantime, Peyton attended the meeting at the office, and she was filled in on the case. She felt that they had a good chance of winning. Her father and the guys had already done a lot of work on it. The case wasn't set to go to trial for at least a few months. This would be more than enough time for Peyton to familiarize herself with the small details and interview the opposing team as well as coworkers of the deceased. Peyton told her father that she was going back to the firm temporarily. Needless to say, he was very excited when he found out, and the news put his mind at ease.

Peyton went over some of the details of the case with her dad while visiting. He gave her all his notes. She got busy working on it immediately; she took to it so well, that it was hard to believe that she even left. Although she, Stanley, and Gabe were working on the case; she wanted to involve one more person. She felt that this would give them the edge they needed, so she called Kimberly. Kimberly had a few clients of her own, but she agreed to work with Peyton.

Unlike Peyton, practicing law is Kimberly's passion. She worked at the Brockington law firm after she and Peyton passed the bar. After getting a better offer and a chance to make partner, she left. Kimberly's a corporate attorney working for Whitmore, Roth, and Moss, a top law firm in Memphis. Her last name, which is Connor, was added after she'd made partner. She's driven and will stop at nothing to get what she wants or what she feels she deserves. She doesn't take 'no' for an answer. It's either her way or the highway.

She grew up in a wealthy household. Her parents were a little freer than the average parents. They allowed her to make a lot of her own decisions and live the life that she wanted. Kimberly would often take drinks from her parent's liquor cabinet. She always did what her parents expected; this way, they wouldn't be on to her. Her parents didn't bother her as long as she appeared to be doing the right things. As a teen, she had secrets that she kept from them, which included her sex life. She often indulged in risqué activities, and she partied hard and lived life as if there was no tomorrow.

Now that she's older, she still enjoys drinking and partying, but in moderation. She was dedicated to her work, and she allowed nothing, not even her partying, to interfere with that.

Kimberly was excited about this case because it allowed her and Peyton to hang out together. Something that Kimberly had been wanting for a while. When Peyton got married, she devoted her time to her husband. This had Kimberly feeling a little left out. She poured herself into her work even more to numb the pain of not having anyone in her life. Due to her aggressive nature, she didn't have many friends because people found her too difficult. Although she had a few associates, Peyton is her closest friend. She's the only person who could not only tolerate her, but she actually enjoyed her company.

One Month Later……

Peyton and Kimberly were at Peyton's home working on the case. It was ten p.m. They'd been working late because it was the only time Kimberly could devote time to the case and stay abreast of her own client's cases. They would begin around six p.m. and end around ten or eleven-thirty nightly. When bedtime came, Peyton would be so exhausted, that all she could do was sleep. She was spending more time at the firm and had begun taking on other responsibilities there as well. She shifted her church activities to others. She thought, *"This is one of the reasons I left. It's so demanding."* She had no extra time to devote to the things she loved. Spending quality time with Gil began to take on a whole new meaning.

On Sunday morning, Gil had to practically pull her out of bed for church, which never happened before. She was always the one up bright and early, especially when the time came for church. Normally after service, she and Gil would go out to dinner, but Peyton wasn't feeling up to it. She wanted to go home and get a little work done. When they made it home, she immediately went into the study to work. About an hour later, Gil went in to check on her. He walked up behind her and began caressing her shoulders.

"Honey, why don't you put that away and come spend a little time with me," he said while giving her soft kisses on her neck. His kisses were soothing, but it wasn't enough to make her put away her work.

"I want to baby, but I have a lot of work to get done by tomorrow. I need more time to prepare for these depositions. I'm already running a little behind the deadline. Sorry babe, take a rain check?" she asked, hoping that he'd understand. Gil was persistent.

"Honey, I love you and told you that if you wanted to return to the firm, I'd support you, but I think you're taking on too much. Since you've been back there, you have been working nonstop. You don't have to work so hard. I know you're doing all of this for Pop. I understand, but you must slow down. I don't want to lose my wife to this." Gil had been feeling neglected. Peyton wasn't cooking for him anymore; they barely made love, and she was too tired to give him the attention that she once had.

"Baby I promise that I'll slow down as soon as this is over. I didn't know that this case was going to take up so much of my time, but if I want to win this thing, I must work hard. Besides, Daddy has already put in so much work, and I owe it to him to give it everything that I have. This means so much to him. After this case, I promise I'll let the guys at the firm handle everything, and our lives will go back to normal."

She pulled him close to her, and they shared a passionate kiss. She was almost tempted to spend a little time with him, but she ended their embrace so that she could get back to work.

"Come on honey; spend a little time with me. I need you, baby."

"I can't right now, and besides Kimberly is already on her way."

"Okay," he said disappointingly. He gave up and went to watch the sports channel. Kimberly came by, and again, they worked well into the night. When they were done, Peyton went to get in bed. When she got there Gil was already asleep. She felt bad for not spending time with him. She pecked him on the cheek and went to sleep.

The next morning, Peyton called the chef to order breakfast. Then, she laid Gil's clothes out for the day. After getting dressed, she went downstairs to eat breakfast with Gil.

"Good morning, honey," Peyton said, kissing him.

"Good morning baby; how did you sleep last night?"

"Not well," she said.

"Well, I noticed you tossed and turned most of the night, what's on your mind?"

"Oh, nothing; it's just something that Kimberly found last night that could be a potential problem, so we have to call a meeting with everyone else and see what can be done about it. I'm just glad this case comes up for court in a few months, and it will be over."

"Not necessarily," Gil said. "Have you given thought to whichever side wins, the other will probably file an appeal, and that starts the ball rolling all over again?"

"Well, let's just keep our fingers crossed that that won't happen." Gil was beginning to sound like a broken record. Peyton changed the subject.

"So, what do you have on your agenda for this week?" Peyton asked.

"I wanted to talk with you about that. I've been asked to a speaking engagement on Tuesday and Thursday of this week."

"Are you planning on speaking?"

"Of course, I'm planning on it. I'm honored to speak. I wanted to know if you would attend with me." Whenever possible, Peyton would go with him when he had speaking engagements or lectures.

"I'm sorry baby, I don't think that I'll be able to make it."

"Well, can you at least try to make it for me?

"I won't make any promises, but I'll try."

After breakfast, Gil left for the clinic, and Peyton went to her parents' home. When she got there, she found her mom in her sewing room. She went in to speak to her, and she plopped down on a chair next to where she was working.

"Hey Mom"

"Hello there"

"What are you making over there?"

"I'm making a dress for the pastor's wife for their anniversary. I'm also making myself a little something cute for the Honors Gala that the mayor is hosting."

"Oh, Mom, I almost forgot about that. Thank goodness that you reminded me. I have to go out and get something to wear. I've been working so much lately."

"I know; you've been working too much on that case; you've neglected your duties at the church and from what Gil says, at home as well."

"Mom, I know that I've been working a lot, but I have to if I want to win."

"Winning isn't everything. It's okay to work hard, but not at the expense of your family, your health, or your happiness. I tried telling your father that, he seemed like he was going to work himself into an early grave. You must set some limits and boundaries for yourself. You must know when to say when, or you could be laid up in a hospital room, or wake up one day and find that everyone that you love is gone because you neglected to set some priorities for your life. That's what I have practiced all my married life. I've had the chance to work with some of the top designers in the world, but I knew that doing so would take me away from my husband and my child, and I was not willing to sacrifice my family. So, I began to create my own designs, and I sell them in my store, and now, thanks to the internet, I ship dresses all over the world from my website."

"Yeah, but Mom, don't you ever wonder what it would've been like to have the fashion world at your feet?"

"I've thought about it, but my family is what matters most to me. I felt led to stay here and care for my family. I'm happy and my life turned out great. If I had the choice to do it all over again, I wouldn't change a thing. Gil needs you. He calls me often worried about you and hoping that maybe there is something I can say to convince you to slow down. Look at how this case is affecting your life and your marriage. Everything will work out fine, and your father will understand. He didn't win every single case, and if you don't win this one, it won't be the end of the world.

"Okay Mom," Peyton said, getting up from her chair. "You're right. I'll keep that in mind. Where's dad?"

"Your father is back in his game room hitting at that old golf ball."

"I'm going to go back and see him for a minute." Peyton went to find her father. When she went in to visit with him, much to her surprise he gave her the same spiel that her mom gave about overworking and neglecting her home. She thought surely that he would understand. There she was, standing in front of him, feeling like a teenager being scolded by a dad for breaking curfew. She allowed her father to finish his speech. She reassured him that she would take it easy. She kissed him and left.

Kimberly and Friends

Kimberly was taking the evening to let down her hair and enjoy herself with a few of her girlfriends. She was at one of her favorite bars and ordered vodka all night. She'd already drunk several drinks, but since she was with her girls, she felt that she would be okay. Her friends Rebecca, Dawn, and Shawna were enjoying themselves. Dawn doesn't drink all that much. Shawna drinks like a fish; she'll drink anything that she can get her hands on, and Rebecca is a social drinker, but she can toss a few back, given the right situation. They were enjoying the night when Kimberly looked up and noticed a gentleman heading to their table. He was a well-dressed guy, and although he was very short in stature, he walked with extreme confidence. As he was on his way, Kimberly said,

"Now, will you look at this shit! I know he's not coming over here." Dawn looked up at him and said,

"I don't know, Kimberly; I think he's kind of cute." Kimberly, looking at him unimpressed, said,

"Cute hell, he looks like a damn dwarf!" They all laughed. He walked up to the table and introduced himself to them.

"Hi ladies," he said with an air of confidence, "I'm Kenneth, and you are?" he asked, looking at Kimberly.

"Uninterested," she said sharply.

"Oh, I'm sorry," he said. "I'm not trying to spoil your evening. Sorry to have bothered you. I just saw a few beautiful women, and I thought that I would come over to meet you."

Dawn, feeling kind of bad for him introduced herself. "I'm Dawn," she shook his hand; this is Rebecca, Shawna, and Kimberly."

"It's nice to meet you," he said shaking the rest of the women's hands.

"So, what are you ladies drinking?" he asked, intending to buy them all drinks.

"We're okay," Dawn said. She knew Kimberly wasn't feeling him, and she wasn't having it. Everyone there wanted to please Kimberly. If there's an alpha female, she would be it. Although she was overbearing, Kimberly was the generous host who always treated her friends when out and they were the followers who were always gracious to be allowed to trail along, each of them for their own personal gain. They were mere groupies, standing in line for the latest handout that Kimberly was issuing. Their reward for being in her circle consisted of fancy trips, shopping sprees, spa visits, exclusive restaurants, clubs, and other benefits. Kimberly looked at him angrily. She felt that Kenneth's visit was an unwelcome intrusion. He quickly got the picture and said,

"Okay ladies, it was nice meeting you."

"It was nice meeting you too," the other three said simultaneously. He walked away from the table.

"I don't know why you encouraged him by making him feel that he stood a chance with any of us at this table," Kimberly told Dawn.

"I was just trying to be nice," she said.

"It must've taken a lot of courage for him to come over to a table full of women and strike up a conversation. I didn't want him to feel that he was wasting his time."

"You see, that's your problem Dawn. You're too nice. I don't give a damn about his courage or his ego. I just tell them how it is, and they get the hell out of my face."

"Well, everybody knows that you're hard on men anyway, so the poor guy didn't know what he was in for when he came over. I just wanted to soften the blow for him."

"To hell with him and his feelings," Kimberly said. "He'll be alright." They continued to drink. Kimberly was tossing the drinks back. Rebecca was a little concerned for her.

"Don't you think that you need to slow it down a little?" she asked Kimberly.

"I came here to enjoy my evening and that's what I intend on doing. Besides, I'm going home with you tonight. Dawn can take my car and keep it at her place. I'll be okay."

"I've got your back," Dawn said. "I know you do," Kimberly told her.

"I thought that you were spending the night with me," Shawna said to Kimberly.

"I was going to, but I changed my mind. I want to go to Rebecca's place tonight. I'll get with you next weekend."

"I was looking forward to having you over. I had my heart set on it. I even have all of your favorite things prepared for you just the way you like it."

"I'll still be able to enjoy them next weekend, right," Kimberly said. Shawna, looking a little disappointed, said,

"Yes, I guess so."

She didn't want to press the issue for fear of angering Kimberly.

"Take Dawn home with you tonight," Kimberly said. "I am sure that you two can find something fun to get into."

"I'm okay," Shawna said forcing a smile on her face. Shawna started gathering her things to leave.

"Ladies, I'm going home now so I can get a little sleep."

"Are you going to be okay to drive?" Dawn asked.

"Yes, I'll be okay." Shawna left. Dawn hung around for a few more minutes.

"Come on Kimberly, I need to get you out of here before you overdose on vodka," Rebecca told her. Kimberly was inebriated, but she was still able to walk on her own. "I'm okay; I still have my faculties about myself." Rebecca placed her arm around Kimberly's waist to help support her so she wouldn't fall and walked her to her car. They left for Rebecca's place.

Chapter Four

THE LECTURE

It was Tuesday morning, and Gil was still in bed. Peyton had been up all night working. She woke before Gil, got dressed to go to the office, and woke Gil.

"Honey, wake up," she said, shaking Gil on the shoulder.

"Shouldn't you already be getting ready for the clinic?"

"Have you forgotten I have the lecture today?"

"Is that today? I thought that was next week."

"So, I guess that means that you won't be there today, huh?"

"I'm sorry honey, I can't." Gil rolled over and pulled the covers over his head. Peyton looked at him and said, "Honey please, don't do this. I'm truly sorry. I will try to make it to the one on Thursday."

"Don't worry about it. I'll be okay." Peyton looked at him, apologized again, and she left. She didn't take the time to eat breakfast.

On her way to the office, she began to think about her life and how she had allowed the case to take over. Gil and Her parents were right; she had lost herself in this case. Gil was treating her differently. She'd never seen him behave the way he did. He had every right to be upset. She thought, *"I need to slow down. I don't want to lose Gil. He's the best thing that's ever happened to me."* She did want to support him; this lecture meant so much to him, but still, she couldn't help but think that perhaps he was being a little selfish. After all, she'd always supported him and remained by his side, even catering to his every whim. *"Why couldn't he support me this time?"* she thought. She brushed it off and went inside.

Kimberly stopped by the office to chat with Peyton for a while. After she was inside, Peyton closed the door behind her.

"What's up girl?" Kimberly asked. "Why are you closing the door?"

"I want to talk to you for a second in private, and Mrs. Wilson hears everything."

"So, what's up girl?"

"Let me ask you something, do you think that I've been working too much?"

"Is that what this is all about? I thought that you really had something to tell me. You're closing the door for this?"

"No seriously, I want to know your opinion. My parents have been on to me lately and now Gil is angry with me. He wouldn't talk to me this morning. He's upset because I couldn't make it to his lecture."

"First of all," Kimberly interjected. "Gil, of all people needs to be supportive of you. You've stood by his side all these years; he really should understand. I think he's being selfish. He's just mad because you're not waiting on his ass, hand, and foot."

"Shhh, you're talking too loud," Peyton said to Kimberly.

"Oh, shut up. She can't hear me. Sure, you've been working a lot, but in this line of work, it takes that, and this case is not just any case. A major corporation has wronged a family, and we must do everything within our power to ensure they get proper representation and are compensated for their loss. We can't do that if we're unwilling to sacrifice a little of our time, and Gil knows that. He's just acting like a spoiled brat. He needs to get his ass somewhere and sit down and be quiet and support his wife."

"I thought that way for a minute," Peyton told her, "I love Gil and want to be there for him. I understand where he's coming from, but he promised to support me. Now, all he's been doing lately is telling me that I work too much. What should I do?"

"You should remind him of his promise to support you and continue to do what's in your heart. When you finish this case, you can go back to being his private nursemaid. You should've known better than to marry a momma's boy anyway." Peyton twisted her face and tilted her head slightly, looking at Kimberly as if to say she disapproved of her comments.

"Kimberly, you don't have to be so hard on him. It's not like that."

"Yes, it is," Kimberly snapped.

"As long as you were his little servant girl, he had nothing to say; once he realized your life doesn't revolve around him and his needs, he can't seem to handle it."

"No Kimberly, I think you're wrong."

"Am I? Then why are we having this conversation? If he truly supports you, would he be treating you this way?"

"He's only concerned about me."

Kimberly handed Peyton a folder. "I came by to give you these ideas that I came up with from what we found last night. Take a look at it and let me know what you think. I've got to go. Keep your head up. I love you, girl. I'll see you tonight."

Kimberly left. Peyton sat at her desk. She threw the file that Kimberly gave her over to the side, leaned back in her chair, and began to think of the conversation with Kimberly. "Well, there's *no time for thinking. It's back to work.*"

By now, Gil was at the lecture hall. He made it there a little early to brush up on his notes. While looking up from his notes, he noticed a very beautiful young woman walking in his direction.

"Dr. Wilkes?"

"Yes, I'm Dr. Wilkes." She held her hand out to shake his.

"Hi, Dr. Wilkes. My name is Rebecca Morgan." He shook her hand.

"It's good to meet you, Ms. Morgan." With her hand lingering in his, she said,

"I'll be attending this lecture today. I'm an admirer of your work. I've read a lot about you." She began to chat with him for a few minutes. She inquired about a possible internship at his clinic. After discussing the subject further, Gil gave her his card.

"Call me when you're ready," he said. He noticed that she was a little flirty. He was used to younger women coming on to him, and he wasn't moved by it.

"I happen to know an acquaintance of yours," she said.

"Who is that?"

"Kimberly Conner."

"Oh yes, she is my wife's friend. How do you know Kimberly?"

"She and I are good friends," Rebecca told him.

"Okay," he said. They continued to talk about the internship and the medical profession for a few more minutes while people began filling the auditorium.

"When did you plan on doing your internship?"

"I was hoping right away."

"Who else have you considered doing your internship with?"

"Well, to be honest, your clinic is the only one I have seriously given any consideration to. I spoke with Kimberly and asked her to speak with you on my behalf. She said she would, but I guess it slipped her mind. She's been very busy lately. I hardly ever see her. She said something about an important case that she's working on."

"I know that all too well. She and my wife are working on the same case. It's that big Hemingway wrongful death case." Gil, figuring that he and Rebecca had something in common and Rebecca had made such a good impression on him, said,

"Answer me this: are you serious about doing your internship at my clinic?"

"Yes, I am."

"Well, I'd like to discuss it a little more with you soon. Are you okay with that?"

"Yes," she said enthusiastically.

"When can you have all of your information?"

"I already have it in my portfolio. I knew that you would be speaking today, so I camped out to wait for you.

Maybe you can take a look at it in your spare time and let me know what you think."

Gil thought Rebecca was beautiful. He pretended not to notice her cleavage as she leaned over to get her information from her briefcase. He noticed that she was all natural. Most of his clients were paying for the perfect cup size, and she had it all. She was flawless. She had a beautiful face, wonderful full breasts, and a small waistline. The white jeans she was wearing hugged her hips tightly. Her buttocks were perfectly rounded, leading to thighs that were unlike anything he had ever seen. He took the file from her, and she handed it to him seductively. He hoped she hadn't noticed that he'd been looking at her breasts. He quickly tried to make eye contact.

"I promise I'll look it over." He placed it in his briefcase and went on into his lecture.

Rebecca was sitting in the audience, awe-struck and hanging on to his every word. She was smitten with him.

Gil is a little over six feet tall with a golden-light complexion. His physique, although not extremely muscular, is well-cut. He's a handsome guy but not the pretty boy type. He wears a goatee, and he keeps his hair shaved in a very low cut. His hair is naturally wavy. He was wearing a nice navy-blue suit with a mild blue tie. He wore his Rolex on his right wrist and a platinum bracelet on his left. He didn't want to appear too dressy because he wanted his audience to focus on his message rather than his attire. He looked great. While speaking, thoughts of Peyton ran through his mind. He wanted her there. He thought to himself, "*She hasn't missed any of my lectures.*" He struggled with the thought in his mind, trying to keep the focus on the task at hand and his notes. He looked at the audience and noticed Rebecca with her hand raised. He called on her. She continued to show interest in his speech by constantly interacting with him, asking questions, and taking notes. Gil was impressed with how knowledgeable she was about his work. Once the lecture was over, she immediately went to Gil to talk with him more.

"I'm impressed," Gil said to Rebecca.

"You're knowledgeable about the medical profession. I better watch myself before I'm out of a job."

"Oh no," she laughed flirtingly. "I told you, I admire your work, and I hope to become a great plastic surgeon like you. I even plan on completing my residency at

Brookhaven Medical as you did. I have one year of schooling left, and then I can go for it."

They continued talking for several more minutes. Gil ended his conversation with her.

"I have to get going. I have another appointment," said Gil. He didn't have another appointment; he was ready to leave. "I'll look over your information and I'll get back to you soon."

Gil left the lecture hall feeling a little down. He walked to his car. He wanted to call his wife, but he felt that she would probably be too busy. He'd left his phone in the car during his lecture. He saw that he had a missed call from her. He called her back hoping that he could take her to a late lunch. He felt a sense of guilt for the way he'd treated her earlier. He wanted to apologize and make it right with her. Her cell phone went straight to her voicemail, so he called the office. The phone rang twice. Mrs. Wilson answered the phone...

"Brockington and Associates, how may I direct your call?"

"Hello, Mrs. Wilson,"

"Hello, Mr. Wilkes."

"Is my wife available?"

"I'm sorry, but she's in a meeting, baby; I'll have her call you when she's out."

"No, don't worry about it Mrs. Wilson; I'll catch her at home. Thank you, Goodbye." Gil hurried and ended the call with her. He was disappointed.

He stopped by the clinic for a while. His receptionist greeted him.

"Dr. Wilkes, I wasn't expecting you in today."

"I hadn't planned on coming in today. I just stopped by to grab a few things."

"You have a few messages." She handed Gil his messages. To his surprise, Rebecca had already left a message, but he couldn't be bothered with that at the moment. He wanted to talk with his mother. Whenever he was feeling down or needed advice, he'd call her. In a sense, Gil *is* a momma's boy. He was an only child. His mom was a stay-at-home mom and housewife. She had been hands-on with Gil in his youth. She was always there nurturing and raising him. Any problem that he had, he would always run to her, and she would somehow fix it. It's no wonder he married Peyton; she was a beautiful younger version of his mother. His mother is a wise woman. She could give sound advice to anybody in any situation, and it seemed that she was always right. He thought to himself, *"I could sure use her wisdom and a little of her special pound cake with ice cream."* He called her.

"Hello, Mom," he said as he cleared his throat.

"Hi, son. It sure is good to hear from you."

"I know that I haven't called you in a couple of days."

"Try a couple of weeks baby, but who's counting?"

"What were you doing, Mom?"

"Oh, nothing. I was just sitting here reading my Bible. I'll be going to Alvera's house later for our bridge game." Gil hesitated for a second, wondering if he should stop by since she would be leaving soon.

"Can I stop by for a minute?" Gil asked, almost sounding like a little boy.

"Of course, you can."

"Well, I'll be there in a minute."

Gil drove to his parents' home. His mother knew something was bothering him because he called her in the middle of the day, and he wanted to come over. He made it to his parent's home. They lived in a beautiful three-bedroom house in a gated community. His parents purchased this home ten years prior at Gil's request. The old neighborhood where Gil grew up had changed. It was no longer the upscale neighborhood that it once was. All manner of people were moving in.

Gil was concerned for his parents' safety, so he got them to move to this home. He drove up to the gate and punched in the code. He used his key to the entry door of the house. His mom was sitting in the dining room at the table, still reading her Bible. He went over and hugged her. He went to the kitchen for a slice of pound cake but didn't see any. "Hey ma, where's the pound cake?"

"Your dad ate it all. There should be some shortbread cookies in the cookie jar. He got a few cookies and a glass of milk, and he went and sat with his mother.

"So, what's bothering you son?"

"What do you mean, Mom?"

"Boy, don't play with me; I can tell somethings on your mind. What is it?"

Gil told her everything that was bothering him. After he had finished, he sat back in his chair and waited for her response.

"Well son, I think you need to be a little more supportive of your wife. She's a good woman. She's not staying away from you because she's having an affair or partying with friends. She's doing what she's supposed to be doing by helping the family. She loves her father and she's concerned about his well-being. Now, I know it must be tough for you, but you must stand behind your wife. You said yourself that it's only temporary. Your wife has stood by you, and she's always supported you in everything. She even sat with me and took great care of me after I had hip surgery. You didn't even have to hire a nurse to look after me. She wouldn't hear of it. She's a great woman. Every mother wants a daughter-in-law like her. Now if you truly love her, you'll stop attacking her attempt to help her family and support her."

"I know mom, all I'm saying is she's working entirely too much, and she's not taking care of herself."

"What you mean is she's not taking care of you."

"Well, I have to admit, that's a part of it. I know it's a little selfish of me, but I miss my wife."

"Well, why not do something nice for her. Have you tried that?"

"What do you mean mom?"

"Plan something to let her know that you care and that you're thinking of her. She's still a woman, and *trust* me, she'll take time out to smell the roses if you know what I mean?" She winked at him. He got up and hugged her.

"Okay, Mom!" He knew his mother was right. He couldn't believe that he hadn't come up with the idea himself. He knew exactly what to do. After chatting with her for a while, he left. He needed to do something nice for his wife to show his appreciation and support. He thought the idea of a romantic weekend getaway would be nice. He called the travel agent. They couldn't go far because of their schedules. He planned a getaway where they could charter a jet and be home the following Monday morning. He ordered roses and had them sent over to her office. Also included, was an invitation to meet with him for a romantic evening in their home. He ordered more flowers and had them delivered to their home. He then drove to the jewelry store and bought her a beautiful pendant and diamond earrings.

He called again, finally reaching her. She thought he was still upset with her, so when she heard his voice, and he sounded happier than that morning, it caught her a little off guard. She was happy to hear from him, and his upbeat mood was reassuring to her.

"Hi honey"

"I was just calling to check on you," Gil said. "How are things going with you?"

"Things are finally winding down a bit around here." While they were talking, the delivery man came into Peyton's office to deliver the flowers. "Oh honey, you're so sweet," Gil heard.

"I love you, baby." Peyton read the card. In it, Gil apologized to her for him being a jerk, and he begged her forgiveness.

"Yes baby, we're okay. I'll be home early tonight." Peyton wanted this night with him. She needed it. She was excited about their evening. She got off the phone and called Kimberly. She canceled her plans with her for the night. Gil rushed home to make sure that everything was in order. The scenery was romantic. Soft jazz music was playing in the background. They had dinner by candlelight. Gil served her. While she was eating her dessert, he excused himself from the table and went to run her bath water in their Jacuzzi tub. He placed scented candles around the tub and rose petals and scented oils in the bath. Warm towels were folded and ready for her. He went back to where she was, and he took her by the hand. They shared a dance. As he danced with her, he turned her around with her back to him. He began to kiss her ear, working his way down to her neck. She melted in his arms. He then pulled the necklace from his pocket and placed it around her neck.

"Oh honey, It's beautiful." She turned and kissed him passionately. Gill pulled the earrings from his pocket and said,

"These little guys began to feel a little lonely sitting in the store without their friend, so I brought them along to keep the necklace company." Peyton was pleased. She put the earrings on with Gil's help. They kissed, and he took her hand and led her into the bath area.

"Oh Gil, this is so romantic." He helped her in. He bathed her and massaged her gently kissing her all over.

She was in a heavenly state of mind. Her body began to relax as she gave in to his sensual touches; she yearned for him, and her anticipation grew stronger with each kiss.

He lifted her from the tub and dried her body. He carried her to their bed, where he rubbed her body with warm oil. The aroma of the candles filled the air as the candles caused the room to glow. He continued to massage his wife. Peyton began to drift off to sleep. He gently kissed her on her neck, she opened her eyes, and she felt a sense of guilt. All the effort that he put into making her night special, where she was dozing off. She fought her sleep. She was on her back, placed her arms around her husband, and gave in to him. They loved each other until sleep claimed them both.

After waking the next morning, they continued to make love. Peyton canceled her plans for the entire day. Gil had a couple of patients that he needed to see, so he had to go in for a while, but he was soon home again, and he joined his wife, who was sleeping when he made it. He slipped into bed with her, and he held her as she slept. She finally woke after about an hour.

"Hi baby," she said to Gil. He kissed her lips and smiled.

"What time is it?" she asked.

"Don't worry about the time, you just rest." She was fully awake, and she didn't want to rest; she felt herself wanting him, and they began to make love again. They enjoyed each other for the rest of the day, preferring to eat their meals in bed. They took a little break from making love. Gil felt that this was the time to ask her to go on the trip he'd planned. He got the tickets and handed her the envelope. She opened it to find the reservation for their weekend getaway. She was ecstatic. She placed the envelope and its contents on the nightstand. She climbed on top of him and started loving him again.

"Oh my goodness; you're going for a record today baby," he said.

"I'm just making up for lost time. I'm loving my man. Why? Can you handle it?" she asked playfully.

"Bring it on baby. I can handle all that you can bring sweetie."

Chapter Five

HARD AT IT

It was late morning and Peyton's sleep was interrupted by the housekeeper. She lightly knocked on the bedroom door. She didn't expect that Peyton would be home because by now she was usually awake or had already gone to the firm.

"Hello Mrs. Wilkes," she said looking shocked that Peyton was still in bed. Peyton looked at the clock.

"My goodness, it's going on ten o'clock."

"I'm sorry to bother you, Mrs. Wilkes," she said nervously. "I thought that you were already gone for the day. I'll come back later."

"Oh, don't worry about it, Jan; I was supposed to be up a couple of hours ago."

"I saw Mr. Wilkes leaving this morning and I assumed that you'd left also." The housekeeper looked around the bedroom and noticed dirty dishes, wine glasses, and clothing on the floor. The room needed a little attention after the couple's night at home.

"Go ahead and take those things with you." After she left, Peyton got up to go to the restroom. When she got out of bed, she looked at Gil's side of the bed and noticed a note from him on the pillow. She read it and smiled. She showered and put on her robe. As she was seated, she got her cell phone to check for messages. Kimberly had called as well as Stanley from the firm. Her mom called to remind her of the upcoming mayor's ball. She called the office to check-in. Afterward, she called Kimberly. Kimberly answered.

"Well, hello, stranger. Where have you been for the past couple of days?"

"Hi Kimberly."

"I've been calling you like crazy. Is everything okay?"

"Everything's fine. I just took some time off with Gil."

"Well, I'm sure he enjoyed that, huh," Kimberly said in a nasty tone. "I'm pretty sure he just loved it when you dropped everything just to cater to him."

"Aww, come on now, Kimberly; I have been neglecting him. We needed this time together."

"So, he made you feel guilty enough to spend it with him, I see."

"No, actually, he was quite sweet about it. He was so romantic. It was beautiful." Kimberly didn't want to hear about Peyton's time with Gil, so she made up a quick excuse not to.

"I really can't talk long; I have a couple of meetings. When are we going to meet for the case?"

"I don't know," Peyton said. "I'll let you know later; Call me when you're done with your meetings."

They ended their call. Peyton was in a lazy mood. Due to the constant lovemaking, she was low on energy. She decided to take another day for herself with no intention of going to the office.

The Intern

It had been two weeks since Peyton and Gil's romantic time together and she was back in the full swing of things. Gil was back at work as well. Seemingly, his patient list went through the roof after he ran a set of new television commercials, so he was working nonstop. He had a great staff. They were dependable and hard-working. He never had anything to worry about with them. He began to think about his encounter with Rebecca. She made a good impression on him. He decided to bring her on board. He had his administrative assistant research her. He spoke with her professors as well as others in the medical field about her studies. They all had good things to say about her. Her resume was impressive.

Gil took a break in between patients. While lounging on his office sofa, his secretary came in. She startled him when she walked into the room because his mind was elsewhere.

"Dr. Wilkes"

"Yeah, how can I help you?"

"I'm sorry to bother you. I tried to get you on the phone, but I got no answer. That young lady Rebecca

Morgan is on line two. She's been calling all day. Would you like to take it, or should I take another message?"

"No, I'll take it," he said. He walked over to his desk and picked up the phone.

"Hello Ms. Morgan"

"Hello, Dr. Wilkes. Did I catch you at a bad time?"

"No, you're okay," Gil said. "I was going to call you. I have some news that you may be interested in." Rebecca began to squeal with excitement hoping that Gil was going to tell her that he chose her for the internship.

"What is it Dr. Wilkes?"

"I'm considering you for the internship."

"You are?"

"I sure am."

"Wow! Thank you so much, Dr. Wilkes. This is a dream come true. I'd be working with one of the best plastic surgeons in the field."

"It's a paid internship. Get ready for a lot of hard work and long hours."

"Oh, I'm already prepared. I'm excited."

"I believe that you're the best person for this internship."

"I thank you, Dr. Wilkes. I won't let you down."

"Okay. I have to go now. My assistant will be in touch with you with the details. I'll talk with you soon."

Gil ended the call. He was satisfied with his decision and took a quick nap before seeing his next patient.

It was a big night, and local celebrities, politicians, and the news media were expected to attend the gala. The event was being recorded to be shown the following night on Access TV.

Peyton was out getting the final touches together for her eveningwear and she was struggling to meet her schedule. Her stylist was at her home waiting for her. Her phone rang constantly. Gil was already home getting dressed. Peyton was so busy helping everyone else, that she had put her things off until the last minute. She finally made it home, and her stylist fixed her hair and make-up, and then her team helped Peyton with her wardrobe. After they were done with the glamorous makeover, Peyton put on a little of her favorite perfume. She appeared to be taking a little too long because Gil was getting impatient. He called the limo around and he ran halfway up the grand marble staircase and yelled for his wife.

"Come on honey. We're going to be late!" Peyton gave herself one last glance in the mirror.

"I'm coming honey," she said, grabbing her purse from the counter. She took the elevator downstairs and left out the side entrance where Gil was waiting for her.

As she stepped into his view, he stopped focusing on trying to get her in the limo and just stood staring at her as if he were meeting her for the very first time. She was wearing a yellow, strapless, evening gown with a small train. The dress was form-fitting, and it hugged her small frame. There was a thigh-high slit, revealing one of her smooth, honey-toned legs. Her beautiful curly hair was in a glamorous updo, displaying a pair of diamond earrings with a matching necklace that set Gil back a pretty penny. She held her crystal-crusted clutch in her hand and smiled at her husband. He was taken aback by her beauty. She was well worth the wait. "Breathtaking!" he said, awestruck. She flashed a flirty smile and said, "I'm ready when you are." Once they were inside of the limousine, he said,

"My love, you look lovely."

"Thank you, honey."

"You're stunning!" he said looking her up and down.

"You will be the envy of every woman at the ball tonight." Gil kissed her on the cheek. She smiled and held his hand.

"I want to hurry and get this night over with so that I can get you home and make love to you. Tell me this Peyton, how am I going to keep my hands off of you tonight?"

"Oh honey, you'll manage. Be a good boy, and there may be a reward in it for you later, okay."

"Well I'll try, but I can't promise you anything."

They made it to the gala. Camera crews were there. A crew was waiting outside their limo. After a brief interview with the media, a young lady led them to their table where they were seated.

The ball was beautiful. Everything was exquisite. The décor was otherworldly. The color theme was champagne, off-white satin, and crystals. The tables were draped with champagne-colored satin tablecloths and crystal dinnerware. Crystal vases were filled with fresh floral arrangements. The chairs were decked out in the same covers that were on the tables.

The local jazz band was a favorite of everyone. Peyton stood at the entrance of the banquet hall admiring the room,

"The mayor went all out on this one honey," she said to Gil. "Everything is beautiful. The ice sculpture is very nice. Everyone looks so nice." While they were looking around, the mayor, along with several other politicians and local celebrities, gave them a warm greeting. Peyton noticed her parents, and Kimberly was also in attendance. They mingled and chatted with other attendees until the ceremony began. The honoree's seats were on the elevated stage. There were twenty in all. Half sat on the right side of the podium the other to the left. While the food was being served, they watched video footage of all the humanitarian causes of the city and those who contributed. Some were wealthy donors; others were honored for donating their time and other resources.

Gil and Peyton's names were called, and they went up together to receive their award. Gil had a speech prepared as always. Peyton said a few words and thanked everyone, including the mayor, and quickly took their seats. Peyton's parents also received an award for their contributions to the community and the honors ball. After the ceremony was over, Peyton and Kimberly worked the room, well mostly Kimberly. While they were on the other side of the room, Gil went to the bar. He ordered a drink and looked around the room. He noticed Rebecca walking up to the bar. She wore a very short black halter dress, so short that bending over was impossible. She was showing so much cleavage her breasts were almost exposed. Every man in the room was watching her. She even gained a few envious stares from the women. She walked up to Gil at the bar.

"Hi Dr. Wilkes," she said. He was shocked to see her there.

"Hello Ms. Morgan. You're everywhere huh?" She laughed.

"I know," she said; "It seems that way. I should say congratulations to you," Rebecca said bowing a little to him.

"Thank you," Gil replied.

"You've made a wonderful contribution to the community. I loved your speech. You're awesome."

"Oh, not really," Gil said taking another sip of his drink. "Just doing what had to be done. My wife is the one who deserves all the credit. She's the one who makes me look good. She's good at handling all of this stuff, and yet they give most of the credit to me. She's the one who makes it all work."

"Well congratulations to you both," Rebecca said in a sarcastic tone.

"Ms. Morgan, what are you drinking?"

"Merlot," she said. Gil ordered her wine and handed it to her.

"Who are you here with?"

"I'm here with Kimberly. Also, the mayor just happens to be my uncle."

"Oh really? Well, aren't you full of surprises I didn't know that. Your uncle's a good man."

"Yes, he's a good man, but I didn't vote for him."

"Oh, come on now," Gil said. "I find it hard to believe that you didn't vote for your uncle?"

"I didn't because we don't share the same political views, but he is a good man. He's conservative. His views are such as turning back the hands of time and sending women and their rights back to the Stone Age. So no, I didn't vote for him. I can't vote for someone just because they're family, right?"

"Well, I don't know," Gil said. "I guess it depends. So, what does your uncle think about you going into the field of medicine?"

"He's happy for me. I told him that I was doing my internship at your clinic. He and my family are happy for me. They knew that I wanted this, and my uncle wanted to talk to you for me, but he decided not to use his influence to help me. He wanted me to get it on my own."

"Well, you did it," Gil said as he held his glass up to toast Rebecca.

"Yes, I did!" Rebecca held her glass up as well. "Thanks to you."

"No, you deserve it. You've worked so hard and your professors had nothing but good things to say about you."

"Oh, so you've been checking up on me huh?"

"Why of course," he said. "You're not the only one who does their homework." They both laugh.

"It's great to have you on board, Ms. Morgan."

"It is my pleasure," she replied. They continued to chat about the medical field. Peyton walked up while they were talking.

"Hello honey!" Gil said to Peyton. She smiled at him. He introduced her to Rebecca.

"Ms. Morgan this is my beautiful wife Peyton."

"Hello Mrs. Wilkes," Rebecca said, reaching out her hand to shake Peyton's hand.

"Hello," Peyton said while shaking her hand and wondering why she was with her husband so long. She'd been watching them from across the room for a few minutes. When she saw Gil hand Rebecca a drink, she decided to go over to see what was going on. Peyton looked Rebecca over. She noticed how pretty she was and she took note of her voluptuous body.

"Honey, Ms. Morgan will be the new intern at the clinic."

"Oh really?" Peyton said looking a little baffled. Rebecca said,

"I was just telling Dr. Wilkes how excited I am that he chose me for the internship, I feel honored.

"Congratulations," Peyton said to her with a forced smile. While they were talking, Kimberly walked up.

"I see you all have met."

"Oh, you know Ms. Morgan?" Peyton asked Kimberly.

"Yes, she's a friend of mine."

"Okay, so Ms. Morgan is a friend of yours?"

"Yes, she is," Kimberly said. Gil tried to break the nervous tension in the air. He saw the confused look on his wife's face. He said, to Kimberly,

"I gave your friend the internship at the clinic; she said that you sent her to us."

"I did," Kimberly said. Peyton looked at Kimberly confused.

"You recommended Wilkes surgery center to Ms. Morgan?"

"Yes," Kimberly said giving Peyton a look as if it wasn't a big deal. At that time, the mayor walked up, and the discussion continued about Rebecca receiving the internship and other small talk ensued. Peyton took Kimberly off to the side to talk with her about Rebecca. She had a few questions, but she mostly wanted to know why Kimberly didn't mention Rebecca to her, before recommending her for a job at the clinic. Kimberly told her that it slipped her mind because she said it had been a few months, and she had forgotten all about it. She said she didn't think that Rebecca would follow up on her recommendation. She told her that it was a surprise to her that Gil gave her the internship, and that she only found out just then. Peyton accepted her answer.

"The next time you decide to recommend a beautiful woman to my hubby, let me know okay." Kimberly laughed at Peyton.

"Okay girl, but you don't have anything to worry about. You said yourself that Gil is a good man."

"He's a good man, not a blind one!" They both laughed and walked back to where Gil and Rebecca were standing with the mayor.

Gil took his wife by the hand and excused them from everyone. He then took her to the dance floor and held her close to him while dancing.

"You are the most beautiful woman here tonight." She laid her head on his shoulder and asked,

"Are you sure about that?"

"Hell yes, I'm sure. I'm the luckiest man alive."

"I guess you didn't happen to notice how beautiful your new intern is or how most of her body parts were popping out of that dress she's wearing. She seems infatuated with you. She was all over you. I noticed her from across the room. She is overly friendly and quite liberal with her hands."

"Honey, you don't need to be worried about that. You're my lady and I see no other woman but you. I love you and I know that you love me, and you don't need to worry about her working at the clinic. I'm not stupid. I love you too much and I love us, and I value what we have together. The love that we share is irreplaceable and nothing's worth losing that. If it bothers you, then I'll rethink this hold internship and recommend her to another clinic."

"No honey," she said. "You don't have to do that. I trust you."

Gil pulled her closer, and they danced and shared a kiss. They enjoyed the rest of their evening at the ball. After the ball, they said goodbye to everyone, including her parents, and they left. Kimberly and Rebecca left the party together and went out for a few more drinks. Kimberly had her limo driver take them back to her place, where Rebecca spent the night. Peyton and Gil went home, where they spent a little time together.

Chapter Six

THE TRIAL AND THE SPLIT

The trial had finally begun on the Hemingway lawsuit, and everyone was confident that they would have great success. The firm worked very hard and long on the case, calling in expert witnesses. They did a great job of presenting their client's case. The trial lasted for several months, and it was time for a verdict. Although a little nervous, everyone remained calm in the courtroom.

Mr. and Mrs. Brockington were there, and Peyton was the spokesperson on that day. The jury found in favor of the Brockington law firm's clients, and everyone was excited. Mr. Brockington went up to his clients and shook their hands. He then went to Peyton.

"Congratulations baby, I knew you could do it."

"Thank you, dad, but you know that I didn't do it alone. Congratulations are in order for everyone here. We all worked so hard. I'm so glad that it's over."

The media was outside waiting for the verdict as well. They interviewed Peyton and Mr. Brockington as well as the clients. After court, they went out to celebrate with their clients at a local restaurant. Peyton was excited about their win. She called Gil at the clinic to tell him about it but she couldn't reach him. It was around three o'clock. Peyton went home and took a shower. Gil called her around five o'clock. She told him about the court case. He congratulated her and he apologized for not being able to be there with her. He told her that he would be working a little late and that he would see her later that night. It wasn't unusual for Gil to work late at the clinic. He can get more done when everybody left the office because he is not bombarded by phone calls and nurses.

She was a little disappointed because she wanted to celebrate with her husband. They said their goodbyes and she went to watch a little television. She watched the news. The Hemingway case was the leading story of the evening. It was on all of the news channels. She called Kimberly to chat for a while, but her phone went straight to her voice mail.

She was in a celebratory mood and she wanted to enjoy this time with her husband, so she decided to surprise him at the office. She prepared steaks and lobster tails. She made a salad. She warmed yeast rolls and stir-fried a few vegetables. She had the housekeeper help her to put the food in food warmers. She got a bottle of wine and some wine glasses and had their driver put everything in the car. While he was doing that, she went upstairs and put on sexy lingerie under a wraparound dress which created easier access. She put on Gil's favorite fragrance and a little makeup, and she was on her way. She didn't call him. When they pulled into the parking lot, she noticed a few cars parked in the lot. Since this was a three-story building, it was filled with many suites that Gil leased to other physicians. There was also a small cafeteria and gift shop inside. Wilkes surgery center was on the bottom right side of the building, it had separate parking for his clients. She had a set of keys as well as a badge to get inside the gate. "Mr. Sam, can you pull around the back? I'm going into the employee entrance. The driver did as she requested. Once parked, he helped her bring the food inside. "Thanks, Mr. Sam. You can go back to the house. I'm going to ride home with my husband. The driver left and she set up the lounge area. Peyton went into Gil's office. Gil had an extravagant office. Peyton designed it herself.

Gil's main office had a glass door that separated the resting area where he would sometimes take naps. It was a small suite. There was a spacious lounge area with a chaise, sofa, and flat-screen television. It had a full bath with a shower. It also had a tiny kitchenette with a microwave and mini fridge. Peyton walked into his office. The lights were out, but the lounge area was dimly lit. She walked up to the glass door and noticed Gil lying on the chaise.

She went inside and walked up to him, and she saw Rebecca on her knees, with her face in his lap. It turns out; that Rebecca wanted more than an internship. She wanted Gil all to herself. She'd been planning to seduce him from the moment she met him, using the internship as a way into his life. She began working on him at the college lecture. She knew well in advance that he would be getting an award at the honors ball, so she arranged to get her tickets in advance from her uncle. She wore seductive clothing to the honors ball, and even more seductive clothing at work. Working at the clinic allowed her to be close to him. None of the other employees cared for her. It was obvious what she was up to, and the other staff members despised her and her antics. She was instrumental in isolating Gil from everyone there, acting as his spoken mouthpiece.

She was always bringing him lunch and coffee and catering to his every whim. She threw herself at him constantly. They were spending a lot of time together. He never took her up on any of her advances. He didn't take her seriously. Many women would flirt with him. It came with the job. But he would always be kind but spurn their advances. Rebecca wasn't going to be easily pushed aside. She was instrumental in breaking up many homes in the past. She felt Gil was no different. No man was able to resist her. The more Gil ignored her, the more turned-on she became. She would stop at nothing to get him even if it meant seducing him, which was what she had planned that night.

As she worked by his side daily, her passion for him continued to rise. Gil felt absolutely nothing for her. He admired her and her seemingly unending commitment to the medical field. His interest in her was purely professional. He loved his wife and there was no question about it.

Rebecca fixed a cup of coffee for him. She pulled a packet filled with a powerful narcotic out of her bra and poured it into his drink. When he drank the drugged beverage, he became drowsy. He went into his office and sat down on his chaise and dozed off. Rebecca then went into his office, and she noticed he was asleep. She went over to him and untied his scrubs and began to perform oral sex on him. Gil was sleeping so soundly that he hardly noticed what was going on. He was startled by her. Looking down at her confused and drowsy, he tried to wrap his mind around what was taking place. He tried to gently push her away, but she worked on him even more. He was naturally aroused by what she was doing. He noticed she'd already taken most of her clothes off. Gil knew they were crossing the line, so he continued to fight her, but to no avail. Whatever she had given him rendered him powerless.

"Stop this, Ms. Morgan!" He finally mustered up a little strength to lift his body from the lounge, but it was too late. Peyton had already walked in on them. Out of anger, Peyton yelled at Rebecca.

"What in the hell are you doing with my husband you tramp!" This shocked Gil. He looked up at Peyton standing over them. Peyton grabbed Rebecca by the hair and pulled her off of Gil. Gil managed to get to his feet. His penis was still exposed, and his pants fell to his knees. "Honey," he cried out to Peyton. Gil pulled his pants up and tightened the string on them. He tried to pull Peyton off Rebecca, but he was too weak. Peyton screamed at Gil. "What the hell's going on? You got this tramp in here giving you a blow job. You're telling me that you're working late. Yeah right! How long has this been going on?" Peyton asked while still wrestling with Rebecca.

"Honey, you've got it all wrong. It's not what it looks like. I was asleep; I didn't know what was going on."

"Bullshit!" She stopped tussling with Rebecca and directed her anger toward her husband. Gil had never heard Peyton use profanity before. Actually, Peyton has never shown any signs of aggression or harsh anger toward anyone. He tried calming her, but it was useless. He looked at Rebecca who was standing behind Peyton with a smug look on her face.

"You need to leave." Rebecca looked at Gil and said,

"Oh, don't act like you didn't know what was going on." Peyton lunged towards Rebecca, but Gil caught her before she could get to her.

"Oh, so you're going to protect this slut!" she said with fury in her voice. Rebecca grabbed her clothes and ran out of the office. Peyton sat on the sofa and began to cry. Gil continued to explain himself, but she refused to believe him. She was inconsolable. She cried for a while and she asked Gil,

"How could you do this to me? How could you do this to us? I trusted you!" She left the office and went into the employee lounge to get her purse. She got her keys, jumped into Gil's car, and drove to Kimberly's place. Kimberly wasn't home so she went to the hotel, where she stayed and cried all night. Gil continued to call her cell phone throughout the night. She didn't want to hear from him. There was nothing he could say to convince her of his innocence. Many thoughts were running through her mind. Her reaction to the situation stunned her. She even began to blame herself for working so much and neglecting her husband. She thought that she should've informed Gil that she wasn't keen on the idea of such a beautiful woman working so closely with him. But many of his clients are beautiful women, *"I wonder how many of them he's slept with,"* she thought. *"Maybe Kimberly was right. I shouldn't have turned a blind eye to my husband."* She truly loved her husband. She'd devoted so much of her life to their relationship and to serving him. She felt it was only natural to love her man in that way. She had never considered her life without Gil. She put all her trust in him. He had never shown any signs or indication that he would be unfaithful. The painful images of Rebecca with her husband continued playing over in her mind.

On the other hand, Gil was sick. He hated himself and felt regret that he had hired Rebecca. He loved his wife and had never considered being unfaithful to her. He went to her parents' home, and he told them everything. Surprisingly, Peyton's parents showed compassion towards Gil. They saw how devastated he was by the events. They knew that he loved their daughter. At that point, all three of them were concerned about her whereabouts and her well-being given the ordeal she had just witnessed. They continued to call her. Her cell phone rang so much that she turned it off. She tried to sleep, but the tears flowed through the night.

With the sun's rising, streams of light shone through the window of her hotel room. The morning was beautiful, but it wasn't a morning made for her. Although it was bright and sunny out, inward, she felt deep dark despair. Her life had changed, and her world, as she knew it, was now over. Nothing felt good to her. She dreaded getting out of bed but pulled herself together to call her parents. She didn't want them to worry. She had no idea that Gil had spent the night at their home. Her mother answered.

"Hey baby, are you okay?"

"No, Mom," she said, her voice cracking, trying not to cry.

"Gil is here."

"He hurt me, Mom," she cried.

"Oh darling," Mrs. Brockington said. "Why don't you talk to your husband? He's been here all night. He's crying and upset. He has been trying to explain what happened. Honey, I think that you two need to talk."

"There's nothing left to say. He made it clear how he felt about me with his actions. I saw everything. I can't get the images out of my head."

"No baby, listen to me," Mrs. Brockington pleaded with her. "Just hear him out."

"Mom, I'm sorry, but I can't right now. I don't want to talk to him."

"Okay, baby," she said, trying to calm her down. I'm not going to force you. I want you to know that your father and I love you, and we want to see you soon."

"Mom, I just called to let you and Dad know I'm alright."

"Hold on a minute baby, your father wants to talk with you before you go." Peyton didn't want to talk with her father. She wanted to get off the phone and cry.

"Hello, baby girl."

"Hi, Dad," she said, sobbing while trying to gain some composure.

"Oh baby, don't cry. Everything's going to be alright."

"Dad, I don't think you understand what's going on. I don't want to talk about it right now."

"I understand, honey. I don't want to pressure you, but I think you two need to sit down and talk. I'm not saying that you need to talk to him right now, but I am saying that you do need to hear him out."

"I'll think about it," she said.

"I love you Daddy. I'm going to go now. I'll call you later." Peyton ended the call. Mr. Brockington hung up the phone and looked at Gil. They knew he made a mistake. "Son, she's not ready. Perhaps you need to give her a little time."

Gil had been a little naïve when dealing with Rebecca. He didn't see her motives. He was just as hurt as Peyton was by what had taken place. He decided to stay at his in-law's place until Peyton showed. She rarely misses a day of visiting her parents. He didn't want to miss her if she stopped by.

Peyton called Kimberly. At least she would understand since her parents appeared to take Gil's side of the story as truth. She waited anxiously as Kimberly's phone rang. She finally answered. She could tell by her voice that she'd been asleep.

"Hey girl," Peyton said to Kimberly. Kimberly could tell that Peyton was upset about something. Kimberly sat up in her bed.

"What's wrong, girl?" Kimberly asked.

"I need to talk to you. I want to come over, can I?"

"Yes girl. Hurry, because I will be heading to the office soon." Peyton left her hotel and drove over to Kimberly's place. By the time Peyton got there, Kimberly was just getting out of the shower. She walked around her apartment nude.

"Wow girl," Peyton said, covering her face. "Aren't you going to cover up a little?"

"What for? We got the same thing. Besides, I'm at home. You act as if you've never seen me naked before. So, what's going on with you? What brings you by?"

She told her friend everything. Kimberly allowed her to cry on her shoulder and apologized to her for her friend Rebecca's behavior.

"I'm sorry," Kimberly said. "I had no idea."

"Oh, it's not your fault; you had nothing to do with that."

"Trust me Peyton, had known that she would pull a stunt like that, I never would've introduced her to Gil. I can't believe that Gil allowed this to happen."

"I know, and I trusted him." Peyton cried.

"I have a few clients to see today, and when I'm done, I'm going to come home, and we're going to spend the day together. I wish I could stay now, but I have to go. I'll be back as soon as I'm done. You stay here. You know where everything is, so make yourself at home." Kimberly went to work. While there, she called a meeting with the partners and let them know that she had an urgent family matter and that she would be taking some time off soon. They were understanding and told her to take all the time she needed and, if she needed anything, to let them know. Over the next couple of weeks, she transferred her clients over to the other partners. She had never taken any time away from the firm. Everyone showed concern for her, and nobody questioned her. When Kimberly got home that evening, she noticed Peyton was still in the same spot as she was when she left.

"Hey Peyton, I'm home." Peyton looked at her with a tear-stained face and swollen, bloodshot eyes. She hadn't eaten anything. She spent the day sobbing. Kimberly went to her side and asked,

"How are you?

"I'm fine," she said with a hoarsened voice.

"No, you're not, and I bet you haven't eaten anything either. I'm going to put on a little soup for you," she said. You need to eat." Kimberly put on some vegetable soup and brought it to Peyton. She forced her to sip a little to keep her strength up. Afterwards, she ran a hot bath. She had to help her bathe because Peyton was too upset and refused to do anything for herself. After bathing, Kimberly massaged her friend and gave her some warm nighttime tea. This seemed to help because she went right to sleep. Kimberly showered and made herself a bite to eat and she went to sleep beside Peyton.

Chapter Seven

THE COMFORTER?

Peyton wasn't talking to Gil or her parents. Gil had camped out at her parent's place daily after work. It had been a couple of weeks, and she was still upset, understandably. Her feelings were raw, and the pain was too great. She refused any thought of reconciliation. She was focused on getting through each day without breaking down. Kimberly was a big help in this area. She was residing at Kimberly's place. That evening, Kimberly brought Peyton's favorite candies, ice cream, and comedy movies. Peyton tried to forget her troubles. She was smiling and having fun with her friend. She was eating again and coming around daily.

Kimberly was a great source of comfort. To take her mind off her troubles, she suggested they take a trip together to the Bahamas. She suggested that they get massages, sit out in the sun, and enjoy life. Peyton was thrilled about the idea. She called her parents to inform them of her plans, but she left no other contact information.

She only told them that she would be in touch. They left a week later.

On their flight, Kimberly ordered a couple of drinks for her and Peyton. Kimberly was nurturing and understanding. Normally Kimberly's harsh and aggressive, but she wasn't that way with Peyton. She catered to her every need. Peyton was comforted by her friend. She thought; *"I could enjoy this for the rest of my life."* Their plane landed.

Kimberly spared no expense. She took care of everything from the limo down to the food details. She booked a three-bedroom, three-thousand-square-foot villa with a private pool and a hot tub. It had floor-to-ceiling windows which showcased the beautiful ocean views. The bedroom had a private terrace that captured the island's picturesque beauty. They had a butler and concierge service, with twenty-four-hour, in-room dining. It was one of the most lavish places. Everything they needed was already in the room. Peyton was impressed. After they got settled in, they went shopping. On their second day, they enjoyed a little sailing and spent a little time snorkeling; they chartered a small plane and toured the other islands.

Kimberly and Peyton seemed closer than ever after being there for a couple of weeks. Peyton used her friend as a crutch as she tried to heal her broken heart. After a day of shopping, they returned to their place for a much-needed soak in the hot tub to soothe their aching muscles. The unending shopping and other activities had taken a toll on them. They sat in the hot tub and talked for a while until Peyton became upset. Kimberly took her inside. She helped her out of her bathing suit and helped her in the shower. Kimberly went into the living quarters of the suite.

When Peyton exited the shower, she handed her a glass of wine and a small pill.

"Here, take this," Kimberly demanded.

"What is this?" she asked.

"It's a little something to help you rest. It's a mild sedative." She trusted Kimberly so she took it.

"I'm going to take a shower, and I'll be right back." Kimberly took her shower, and she put on a comfortable nightie. She was nude underneath. Peyton was lying on the sofa when she got out of the shower. She sat next to Peyton. Peyton eased her head on her shoulder. She motioned for Peyton to lay her head in her lap. She did. She stroked Peyton's hair, and she massaged her temples. By now, the sedative, along with the wine, was taking its effect on Peyton. Kimberly could tell, so she got up from the sofa and led Peyton to the bedroom. She helped her out of her clothes and helped her in the bed. Peyton was feeling good and mellow.

"What kind of pill was that you gave me?" she asked. "I feel so good."

Kimberly said,

"I told you; it is a little something to calm your nerves."

"Well, it's working wonderfully," Peyton said drowsily.

Kimberly knew that Peyton was a little buzzed. She lay beside her and held her while talking to her. Kimberly pulled her over on her back, and she lay by her, stroking her arms. Kimberly's voice was hypnotic as she whispered into Peyton's ear. Peyton was in a euphoric state. She couldn't make out what Kimberly was saying, nor was she trying to. She moved in closer, and she began to kiss Peyton's neck. She waited to see the type of reaction she would receive. Peyton seemed not to notice what was happening to her. She continued kissing her neck. She then gently sucked her on her neck. Peyton began to moan softly. Kimberly took her fingers and traced the outline of her breast one and then the other. Peyton's reaction was positive, so she started to suck her breast lovingly and passionately one by one. Peyton arched her back slightly and indicated that she was enjoying what was happening. Kimberly was excited, and her body began to drip with moisture. She pulled Peyton's panties off and began to explore her body with much passion. Much to Kimberly's surprise, Peyton began moving her hips in a slow rhythmic motion, pressing her pelvis against Kimberly's mouth. This excited Kimberly. She couldn't believe that she was making love to Peyton. Peyton continued to move her hips until she suddenly thrust her pelvis towards Kimberley's mouth with force. She froze and exhaled. Her body went limp. Kimberly knew what happened. She had done this many times before. She slowly lifted her body and climbed on top of Peyton. She kissed her softly on her ear and then her neck. Peyton's breathing was sporadic. Kimberly looked into her eyes. Peyton appeared to be in and out of consciousness.

"Are you okay?" Kimberly asked. Peyton couldn't answer; all she could do was lie there.

Peyton had never experienced anything like it before. She loved it. She was hooked instantly. Gil had never made her body feel like that before. Kimberly was passionate and loving. Kimberly asked,

"Peyton, are you okay?"

"Yes," Peyton replied in a soft whisper.

"What did you do to me?"

"Did you like it?" She didn't answer, she sighed and went to sleep. Peyton woke early the next morning with feelings of guilt. She was still drowsy from the pill that was given to her. Her legs felt like rubber. She got in the shower. Kimberly went into the bathroom to pee. Afterward, she slipped into the shower with Peyton and began washing her body. Peyton thought, *"I can't do this again; last night was a mistake. I don't know what came over me and why I let this happen."* She tried to resist Kimberly.

"I don't think we should be doing this," she said softly, but Kimberly insisted.

"Doing what?" she asked.

"You don't think that I should be doing this?" At that, she knelt and began kissing and circling her tongue around her clitoris. She was persistent. Peyton tried resisting again, but Kimberly worked on her even more. As she continued to perform oral sex on her, she kept asking her,

"Do you really want me to stop?" Peyton mouthed the words,

"Yes, Kimberly this is wrong." Kimberly ignored her and continued until Peyton submitted. She was no longer fighting but participating. *"This should not be happening she thought."* But what was happening to her was like nothing she had ever felt before. They got out of the shower. They didn't dry their bodies but climbed into bed and continued what they had started for most of the morning. Afterwards, they ordered room service. Peyton lay there thinking, and again, feelings of guilt gripped her. Once their food arrived, Kimberly began to talk to her.

"So, how do you feel about what has taken place here?"

"What do you mean?"

"I mean, do you regret it."

"I enjoyed it, but I think that we may have crossed the line. First off, I'm a Christian. I'm not a lesbian. And the second, I'm still a married woman. I don't think that it was right at all. What about our friendship? What does this mean for us?"

"So, you're feeling guilty?"

"Yes," she says. "It's not just that I'm feeling guilty, I mean, I don't know how I feel. I have never slept with anyone other than my husband. I never would've thought that I would've allowed anyone other than him to touch me, let alone another woman and especially not my best friend. My body was feeling one thing, but in my heart, I was... I know that it's wrong." With a stoic expression, Peyton was trying to decipher just what she was trying to convey to Kimberly.

"I would like to say something to you, Peyton. I have a confession to make. I want you to hear me out before you say anything."

"Well, what is it?"

"I'm in love with you. I have been for years." Kimberly went on to reveal her true feelings to Peyton.

"I've tried to suppress my feelings for you all these years. I didn't want to tell you because I didn't know how you would take it. I didn't want to run you off. I thought that I could contain my feelings for you, but last night, while looking at you and knowing what you had gone through, I wanted to express my love for you, and I couldn't help myself. I had to have you. I had to share my passion with you, even if it cost me our friendship."

Peyton was stunned by what she heard. She tried replaying the years of their friendship in her mind to see if she could see any signs of what Kimberly was telling her. Nothing about their friendship made her believe otherwise. Kimberly leaned into her and gently pushed her onto the bed.

"I have to have you Peyton." Peyton had an uneasy feeling about what was about to take place again. Kimberly began to perform oral sex on her again.

"I love you Peyton," she said this in between sucking her and darting her tongue in and out of her wetness.

"I've always loved you, not only as a friend but as my woman. I felt that one day, this chance would come. Do you think that you could ever love me?" Peyton couldn't say a word. She could only enjoy Kimberly's warm mouth and great technique.

Peyton's heart began to beat faster. *"What is going on? What am I doing? What is happening to me? I don't need to be doing this. Will God forgive me?"* Peyton knew in her heart that she shouldn't be engaging in such immoral behavior, but she didn't want Kimberly to stop. Peyton moaned as Kimberly continued,

"But you're my friend," she whispered. Kimberly wanted more than friendship. She teased her a little with her tongue. "I don't want us just to be friends; I want you to be my woman."

"Be your woman?" Peyton asked. That sounded very strange to Peyton. Just as strange as her lying there allowing her best friend to be intimate with her, but this was a strange time and a very foreign place for Peyton, with her husband and Rebecca and her parents. Her life seemed to be spinning out of control. Peyton closed her eyes and tried to focus. Kimberly stopped for a second right at the point of Peyton's orgasm. Peyton placed her hands on the back of Kimberly's head and stroked her hair intimately to say she was grateful and appreciative of the gift her friend was giving. She was coming to a climax that was so amazing that she wanted to enjoy it to the fullest. While she was climaxing, Kimberly gave it her all until again she had her friend in a state of ecstasy that she would never forget. Kimberly loved Peyton's body until she was drained of all her energy and strength, and she was too weak to move. She held her as they both slept. They stayed in the Bahamas for a month. This gave Kimberly all the time she needed to infiltrate Peyton's mind. She was no longer herself and was totally under Kimberly's influence. She controlled her. Kimberly had turned Peyton out sexually, and she managed to forget all about Gil.

Kimberly had always loved Peyton. She was waiting for the right time to pounce. Since it was not happening fast enough for her, she decided to help things along by sending Rebecca to Gil. She wanted to keep him occupied while she held up the Hemingway case so she could spend more time with Peyton. Rebecca was one of Kimberly's lovers. Kimberly promised her that if she played along, she would help her get Gil; in return, she could get what she always wanted, and that was Peyton. The real reason Kimberly couldn't keep a man was that she didn't want one. She's a lesbian. She hated men. She'd been having fantasies about Peyton since college. She was finally getting what she wanted. She wanted Peyton to divorce Gil as soon as possible. Her intentions were for her to move in with her immediately and to start a life together. In her mind, Peyton is already hers. Peyton's not really in love with Kimberly but is confused and hurt. She doesn't realize that she's been set up by her best friend. She soon believed that she was falling in love with Kimberly. Although Peyton feels she's in love with Kimberly, she wasn't ready to engage in public displays of affection.

Kimberly insisted that they travel to Hawaii. She needed more time to work on Peyton mentally. She agreed to the trip. They stayed in Hawaii for close to a month. Kimberly now had her completely under her spell. Peyton allowed herself to be manipulated due to her inability to properly deal with her pain. Peyton was confused about who she was, and what she wanted. She was no longer feeling guilty, and she wasn't praying or reading her bible anymore. While in Hawaii, Kimberly continued to manipulate her. They would be lying on the beach together or somewhere relaxing when Kimberly would begin her spiel.

"I'll never hurt you as Gil did," she'd tell her.

"I've been telling you for years while you were putting all of your trust in him that he was no good. Since you were so in love with him, I just stepped back and let you have it. You know you really should've been with me all along. Look at how much time you wasted on that relationship. And what has it gotten you? A broken heart. I'm a woman, and I know what you need. Men are totally out of touch with women and their needs. A woman can love another woman better than a man can. He doesn't have a female body. He doesn't know what makes her feel good. At best, he can only guess how to satisfy her sexually. I got you baby. I know exactly what you need. I'm going to satisfy you for the rest of your life. I love you Peyton."

By then, Kimberly was telling Peyton she loved her so much that Peyton almost felt a sense of obligation to tell her the same. After all, Kimberly was the only one there to help her in her time of need. What Kimberly had done was help herself to Peyton. Peyton began to treat Kimberly as if she were her mate. This pleased Kimberly. She was now confident enough with their relationship to take her back home.

Chapter Eight

THE RELATIONSHIP

After getting off the plane, reality hit Peyton hard. It was easy for her to forget her pain when she was lying on an island, but now she was home. When she left home, she tried to leave the pain behind her, but now that she's back, she realized it was very much present. Fear overtook her. She grabbed Kimberly's hand as if she could protect her from the fear she felt inside.

"What's wrong baby?" Kimberly asked. Peyton squeezed her hand tighter.

"Oh, come on," she said. "I see what's wrong with you. Let me hurry and get you home. Don't worry about a thing. I told you, I have you now. You are going to be okay."

Peyton didn't feel that she was going to be okay. On the ride to Kimberly's home, she realized she now had two problems. According to her beliefs, she was now in an immoral relationship with her best friend and she knew that this would be a problem for her. Her church life, her parents, and the community in which she served ran through her mind. She knew there was no way of explaining her relationship to them. If she tried, she knew it wouldn't be received well. She'd never practiced immoral behavior or taken any risks in her life. She thought, *"I will keep it quiet for now."* All she wanted to do was get to Kimberly's place and hide in what she believed was comfort and safety from the outside world.

She had developed an unhealthy addiction to Kimberly, and any time she felt pain, she would latch on to her. Kimberly was enjoying this. She'd been obsessing over Peyton for years. It was difficult, but she kept her feelings to herself until she could no longer bear them. She decided to do something about it and went into manipulation mode. After meeting the lovely Rebecca at a party, they developed a sexual relationship. Rebecca had a hot body no doubt. A body that made men ogle. Most men were spellbound by her beauty, and they found her irresistible. It was difficult for guys to turn her down. Kimberly thought, *"Hell, I couldn't even turn her down."* Although Kimberly enjoyed sex with Rebecca, that wasn't where her heart was. Rebecca was bi-sexual, and she would sleep with anybody given the right situation. As long as it benefitted her and brought her pleasure, she was all for it.

After sleeping with Rebecca and developing an ongoing friendship, they began to discuss Peyton and Gil. Due to Kimberly's obsession with Peyton, she often discussed her in conversations with her other friends. When she learned of Rebecca's admiration for Gil and her desire to work with him, it was then that Kimberly began to plot against the couple. If she could get Gil to fall for Rebecca, then she could have Peyton. It was a long shot, but Peyton was worth the risk.

Rebecca jumped at the chance to meet Gil. Kimberly told her that she would set everything up for her. She mentioned that she could get an internship at his clinic. Rebecca was grateful to Kimberly, and they began to hang out even more as the plot unfolded. Kimberly gained control over Rebecca, and she spoiled her by buying expensive gifts and taking her on lavish trips to create a sense of obligation to her.

After arriving at Kimberly's place, Peyton went into the shower. The housekeeper was already there doing her weekly cleaning. Kimberly paid her in advance and gave her the rest of the day off. She didn't want any interference from anyone. She wanted Peyton to feel comfortable enough to be in her home.

While Peyton was still in the shower, Kimberly listened to the answering machine. There was a message on there from Rebecca. She was upset because Gil fired her from the clinic. Kimberly couldn't care less. She had what she wanted, and as far as she was concerned, Rebecca could get lost. There were several messages from Gil. As soon as Kimberly heard Gil's voice, she stopped the message from playing out of fear that Peyton would hear it. He pleaded with Kimberly to speak to his wife on his behalf and have her call him.

"Yeah, like that's going to happen." Kimberly talked back to the answering machine as if Gil could hear her. "She's mine now!" Kimberly went into the kitchen, and although it was early in the day, she fixed a glass of gin and grapefruit juice for Peyton and her.

Peyton wasn't a heavy drinker, but she took occasional glasses of wine with her meals. Since she's been with Kimberly, she's been feeding her more alcohol than she was used to consuming. Sometimes she would give her a mild sedative each time she was feeling on edge. This was one of those days. She went into the bathroom where Peyton was drying off. She handed her the drink and the sedative. By now, Peyton had become familiar with this routine. She took the pill and drank her liquor without incident. This action also helped to keep her detached from reality. As usual, after the drink and the sedative, Kimberly worked on Peyton sexually. Immediately after sex, she began her routine of working on her mentally.

After about a week of being at home and spending time with Peyton, the vacation was over, and Kimberly decided it was time for her to go back to work. Kimberly didn't want any unwanted phone calls from anybody, so she got her home phone number changed. She had a new life and the love that she always wanted. Everything was looking up for her and she wanted no problems.

Peyton got out that day because she was feeling kind of stuffy after being in the house for almost a week. She decided to go by and talk with her parents. She missed them. It had been almost three months since she saw her parents or spoke with Gil. She had been checking in occasionally with her parents while making them promise not to try and talk with her about her marriage. They promised not to bring it up unless she wanted to discuss it.

She stopped by. She was nervous about seeing her father. She could handle her mother, but it seemed like her father could always see right through her. They were happy to see each other. He put no pressure on her. He didn't want her to run off or shut down. He allowed her to be herself. They relaxed and watched television together. They talked about old times at the firm and her childhood. Peyton felt good and happy that she had visited her parents. She went into the kitchen to fix her and her father a snack. On her way, she ran into her mother.

"You know, anytime that you feel that you want to talk, I'm here for you, baby," Mrs. Brockington said to her.

"I know, Mom, and I love you, and I thank you for that." She kissed her mom and continued towards the kitchen. When she heard,

"How's Kimberly doing?" Peyton stumbled.

"Um, she's doing fine, Mom," she said.

"What is she up to these days?"

"Nothing, really," Peyton said.

"She's been looking out for me though. Ever since this happened with Gil, she has taken it upon herself to care for me. Without Kimberly, I don't think that I would've made it."

"Mmm hmm." Her mother cut her eyes at her.

"So, what's her take on all that's happened?"

"Mom, please; not right now." Peyton was nervous talking about Kimberly, and her mother caught her off guard with the questions.

"Tell her to call me. I would like to talk to her, okay."

"Okay, Mom, but what's all this sudden interest in Kimberly?"

"I don't know; she's been on my mind a lot lately and with you two spending so much time together, it could hardly be healthy. She won't even let anybody get close to you. I think that you need to watch her. Something's not right with her. I'm getting some strange vibes about her."

"Oh Mother, you are just being overly cautious. Kimberly has been a great friend, and she has been looking out for me. She loves me. She has my best interest at heart."

"I'm sure she does, but I think that she's been acting a little strangely since all of this took place."

"I'll have her call you, Mom. I've got to get Dad's snack." Peyton hurried and left the room. She wasn't prepared to discuss Kimberly. She even found herself a bit protective of her. She was loyal to Kimberly, and she didn't like her mother's tone about her. She got the snack, sat with her father for another hour, and left. When she got in the car, she called Kimberly. Kimberly immediately answered the phone.

"Hi baby," Kimberly said. Kimberly was in a meeting, and her phone had been set to vibrate in case Peyton called.

"What time are you coming home?"

"What time do I need to come home?"

"Come as soon as possible. I want to see you."

"Are you okay?"

"Yes, just missing you."

"I'm missing you too, baby. I can't wait to get home to you."

"Okay," Peyton said, "I'll see you later."

Peyton drove back to Kimberly's place. She relaxed and watched television. While watching the screen, one of

Gil's ads came on. She couldn't find the remote in time to change the channel. When she saw his face, all the pain came back, hitting her like a ton of bricks. She turned the television off, went into the bedroom, and began to cry. After about thirty minutes of crying, she calmed down and began to think of all the good times that she and Gil shared. She thought about the first time they met. They were at a college rally, and Gil was handing out flyers; he handed her one, not recognizing that she, too, was a volunteer. When she informed him, he apologized.

After their encounter, Gil made it known that he wanted to get to know her. She was interested in him as well. They talked all day. They did not leave each other's side until the function was over. They exchanged information and became friends, and soon after, they began dating. While in deep thought, Peyton began to smile, remembering their wedding day. They had the traditional wedding that most women dreamed of. Peyton's father spared no expense. He felt there was nothing too good for his daughter. Although they had a lavish wedding, all Peyton and Gil cared about was the love they shared and the strong bond between them. They wanted to be alone together to celebrate their union.

They left the wedding reception early, leaving their family and guests to celebrate without them. As she thought about their life together for what felt like hours, it only turned out to be twenty minutes. She loved him, but she was angry at him. She wanted to reach out to him, but it was still too soon.

She checked her voicemail for messages. Gil left mostly all the messages that were there. When she heard his voice, she began crying. He was begging and pleading with her in most of the messages. She finally got down to the last few messages. By then, he just wanted them to meet to discuss their plans for the future. He'd settled in his mind after not hearing from her that he would no longer try to persuade her to come back to him but that they should make plans to talk. She still wasn't ready.

Kimberly made it in from the office. She went into the bedroom, where Peyton was lying on the bed. She noticed she had her cell phone in her hands and tears in her eyes. She thought Peyton had talked with Gil. She looked upset. She dropped her things on the bed, ran around the side of the bed where Peyton was lying, and took the phone out of her hand. Peyton cried on her shoulder.

Kimberly took her shoes off and motioned for Peyton to scoot over and she climbed into the bed with her. She held her while she cried herself to sleep. She took her phone and pressed the recall button to see who she had called last. She was a bit relieved when she didn't see Gil's number. She called her voicemail to see what messages were on the phone. She didn't have her PIN so she couldn't hear the messages. She got a shower and called a Chinese restaurant. She planned on them going out that evening, but she felt that Peyton was too upset to go anywhere. Peyton was awake by the time the food came.

"Hey sleepy head."

"Hey," Peyton said sleepily.

"How are you feeling?"

"I'm feeling better, I'm hungry."

"Would you like to eat in the dining room, or do you want to eat here?"

"I'll eat in the dining room. I have to freshen up. I'll be there in a minute."

"Okay, I'll get everything ready for you." Peyton went into the dining room. She noticed that Kimberly brought her flowers, and she lit candles. She had wine and food sitting there for her. Kimberly kissed her on the cheek and then took her seat.

"The flowers are lovely," Peyton said.

"I didn't mean to ruin our evening. I'm sorry."

"Oh baby, you're okay. You didn't ruin anything. I understand what you're going through. You need time to heal. You've been through a traumatic experience. You've been betrayed by someone who should've loved and protected you, but he hurt you instead. It takes time to heal from something as devastating as that. Have you talked with him?"

"No, I haven't. I listened to my messages today. He left a few."

"Is that what had you upset?"

"Yes, it was a bit overwhelming to hear his voice," Peyton replied.

Kimberly wanted to know if Peyton was considering talking to Gil any time soon. She also wanted to know her feelings for him, so she asked her,

"Are you planning on talking with him about what happened?" Peyton playing with her food and not looking up said,

"I was thinking that I should begin to deal with it. It's been a few months, and I haven't spoken with him."

"Do you still love him?"

"I've always loved him. I've never stopped loving him. Because of his actions, I don't think we could ever reconcile. This isn't what I imagined when we fell in love or when we said our vows. I still can't believe this happened. I thought that he loved me." Peyton began to sob.

"That's because he's a man. They never keep their promises. They're only as loyal as the next sexiest woman they see. Men aren't shit. I've been telling you that all along. You didn't listen to me. You thought that Gil was different, but he's just like the rest of them."

"I know," she said still sobbing; "I should've listened to you. You were right. Somehow, I thought that Gil was different."

"No man is different," Kimberly said.

"They're all the same. I love you, Peyton. I'll never cheat on you, nor will I leave you. You're mine now and I am going to take care of you. No one will ever hurt you again. I'm going to do things for you that you never thought possible. What you need is to begin to think about us and our future together. You need to let go of Gil, and all the pain associated with him, and let's live our lives together. Okay"

"Okay," Peyton said, looking unsure about what she was hearing. "I guess you're right." Kimberly reached across the table and held her hand for a brief moment.

"I know I'm right." She then pushed back from the table and went to her purse to get a sedative for Peyton. She handed it to her. Peyton took the pill and gulped it down with a swallow of wine. Kimberly smiled, got up from her seat, and embraced her. Kimberly led her to the sofa, and they made love. She was into her so much that she hardly noticed the doorbell ringing. Peyton had to tell her that someone was at the door. By now, they were both nude. Kimberly wondered who could be coming by her home unannounced. She didn't bother putting on clothes because she had not planned to open the door. She went to the door and looked through the peephole. It was Rebecca. *"What in the hell does this heifer want?"* She opened the door only a little.

"Yes, what is it?"

"I need to talk to you," Rebecca said desperately.

"About what?"

"Can you let me in?"

"No. I'm busy right now. I'll call you tomorrow."

"This can't wait until tomorrow." All the commotion alarmed Peyton. She got up from the sofa and went to the door.

"Is everything okay?" Peyton asked.

"Yes," Kimberly said. Rebecca peeped through the cracked door. She could see a partially nude Peyton in the background. She figured perhaps Kimberly was sleeping with her. She was a bit jealous and wanted to know what was happening. Kimberly told her to hold on because she saw that Rebecca wasn't going to leave. She went and put on a robe. Peyton couldn't see Rebecca from where she was standing. Kimberly said, "Babe, go and wait for her in the bedroom." After Peyton left the room, Kimberly went outside to talk with Rebecca.

"What in the hell do you want girl?" With a look of desperation, Rebecca said,

"I've been trying to reach you for a couple of months. I tried calling your home phone and it's disconnected. Gil fired me from the clinic."

"What do you want me to do about it?"

"I want you to talk to him for me. But I can see that you're preoccupied with his wife. I guess I'm not the only one who had something up their sleeve." Kimberly reached her hand through the cracked door and put her finger in her face, almost to the point of touching her.

"Look bitch! You don't know what you're talking about. I would advise you to stay the hell out of my business. If you hadn't been so stupid as to let her catch you, then you wouldn't have been in this predicament, huh? Now if you want my help, you'll have to call me tomorrow at my office. We can discuss it then, but if you ever come by here again unannounced, I will beat your ass. Do you understand me?"

Rebecca saw the evil in Kimberly's eyes, and it frightened her. She knew that Kimberly would make good on her threat. She agreed to call her the next day, and she left. Kimberly went back into the bedroom, where Peyton was waiting for her. She lied to her and told her that it was a desperate client. Luckily for Kimberly, Peyton never saw who was at the door. Kimberly lay down beside her. As much as she wanted Peyton, Rebecca had spoiled her mood. Kimberly knew something had to be done about Rebecca, or she would keep coming back. While she was lying there thinking, Peyton placed her arms around her.

"Is everything okay?" she asked. Kimberly stroked her arm while looking aloof.

"Yes, everything's okay. It was one of my clients. She was desperately worried about her case. Everything's okay."

"Are you sure?"

"Yes, I'm sure." Kimberly didn't want her to worry, so she turned her attention back to her to ease her mind.

"Peyton, you know I love you, right?"

"Yes Kimberly, I know."

"But do you know how much I love you?" Peyton didn't know how to answer that, so she said nothing. She asked again. Peyton said,

"No, tell me how much."

"I'll do anything for you. All I want is your happiness. You should never be unhappy for any reason. I'll do any and everything within my power to make that happen. I'll please you in every way possible. Anything you ask of me, I'll do. I want you for the rest of my life. Is that okay with you?"

"Yes," Peyton answered. She held her until she went to sleep. Kimberly couldn't sleep. Everything she'd worked for was being threatened. She thought that having Peyton as her lover would remain an unresolved fantasy, but now that she has her, she's in no way prepared to give her up. Not for anything. Not for anyone.

She plotted ways to handle the situation with Rebecca. She knew that Rebecca was a little off balance. She needed to get with her to get a handle on things. She couldn't take any risks. She was up all night thinking of what she would do.

Chapter Nine

POTENTIAL THREAT

Morning finally came in what seemed like an eternity to Kimberly. Peyton had no idea that Kimberly hadn't gotten any sleep. She was up a little early and fixed breakfast for them both. Kimberly came to the table after showering. "Good morning," Peyton said cheerfully.

"Good morning."

"I made you some French toast, eggs, and bacon this morning."

"I am sorry baby," Kimberly said.

"I don't have much of an appetite this morning. I'll have a glass of orange juice. I must leave a little early this morning. I have a busy schedule. I'll be home a little late today. I have court."

Peyton was all too familiar with an attorney's hectic schedule, especially staying late at the office and researching cases sometimes until the morning. Not to mention the back-and-forth of attending court or meetings with clients.

"Is there anything that I can help you with?" Peyton asks.

"No, I'll handle it, but if I need you, I'll keep that in mind."

Kimberly briefly played with the thought of Peyton working beside her again. But she wasn't going to be in the office all day. She needed to get with Rebecca. Peyton tried to get her to eat, but again she refused. She gave Peyton a hug and a quick kiss on the cheek. She left for her office.

Kimberly went to the receptionist and retrieved her messages. Afterwards, she went into her office and called Rebecca. Kimberly made small talk with her. She apologized for snapping at her. She wanted her to feel comfortable. Kimberly suggested that they meet for lunch. She agreed to meet with Kimberly. They decided to meet at a restaurant that was nearby and convenient for them. When Kimberly arrived, she saw Rebecca's car already in the parking lot. *"Look at this desperate bitch,"* she mumbled under her breath. Kimberly went inside. She saw Rebecca already seated, and she went over to join her. She kissed her on the cheek before she took her seat. This was to make her even more comfortable.

"Hi," Kimberly said, very friendly. "You look fabulous."

"Thanks," Rebecca replied. She smiled at Kimberly.

"So, tell me what's going on."

Kimberly picked up her napkin and put it on her lap. At that, the waiter came over. Rebecca didn't answer Kimberly's question at that time because the waiter was at the table.

"Can I get you something ma'am?" he asked Kimberly.

"Yes, I'll have a cup of coffee."

"I'll have the same," Rebecca said.

"Yes ma'am." The waiter got their coffee. They resumed talking.

"Tell me what's on your mind."

"Well," Rebecca said with a pitiful look on her face.

"After Mrs. Wilkes caught me with Dr. Wilkes, he didn't come to work for a while. I tried calling him, but he didn't answer. I left messages apologizing to him for what happened. He wouldn't call me back. I continued going to work anyway. He finally came in about two weeks later and fired me. He talked to me about the ramifications of sexual harassment in the workplace. He said that he could have me arrested for sexual assault and felony assault for drugging his coffee. I'm still in a panic about that."

"Hold up, Peyton told me that she caught you two. So, what happened?"

"It had been a busy day. We worked with all our patients. After the rest of the staff went home, I took the package you gave me and poured it into his coffee. After he went into his office and lay down, I followed him and did exactly what you told me to do.

At first, he tried to resist, but I continued until he started to relax. That's when Mrs. Wilkes walked into the office and saw us. She went crazy. She grabbed me and started hitting me. Dr. Wilkes pulled her off me. I left the two of them there, and I went home."

"So, what made you try him in the office? You didn't stick to the plan. You were supposed to lure him to your home and seduce him there."

"Well, he was hard to get that way. How was I supposed to get him to my place? He was all about *I love my wife* type of shit, so I had to try him at the office. How was I to know that his wife was going to come there? I didn't mean for her to catch us. I wish things could've gone differently. Anyway, I thought that perhaps you could talk to him for me."

"Now come on Rebecca, you can't be serious. What is it that you actually think that I can say to him at this point?"

"Maybe he's had time to think things through."

"You're much smarter than that. Talking to him now will do nothing to help you out. You see he doesn't want you. I think that losing his wife is hard for him. He probably blames you for this happening. If he fired you and he's not talking to you, then I would think that his mind is made up about you. You should consider moving on with your life. Leave the man alone before he does have you arrested."

"But I was betting on that internship."

"Rebecca, you see the man has moved on. There are other clinics and hospital facilities. You need to try to get an internship with someone else."

"It's too late," she said, looking hopeless. "And even if I could get one at this point, Dr. Wilkes wouldn't give me a reference. What am I going to do?"

"I don't know what to tell you. If there's anything that could be done at this point, then it's going to take some time and patience to figure out. I happen to know that he wants his wife back, but that's not going to happen. She wants nothing to do with him. You may have a chance if you play your cards right." Kimberly was lying to Rebecca. She knew that Gil didn't want her. Rebecca began to question Kimberly.

"What's in this for you? You never told me why you wanted Dr. Wilkes and his wife to split."

"I have my reasons."

"You seem to be benefitting from their breakup. Why would you set up your friend's husband with another woman? Dr. Wilkes doesn't seem like a bad person. His wife seemed sweet enough."

"You know Rebecca, it's funny how you weren't asking questions like this when you were chasing him or when you had his dick in your mouth. Now, because your plan failed, you want to question me. If you had gotten what you wanted out of the deal, would you be coming to me this way?" Rebecca felt ashamed because Kimberly had her on the spot. She held her head down for a second. She looked up at Kimberly.

"I'm sorry for coming to you this way. It's just that I've been feeling deserted after all this happened. I haven't been able to reach you for months. I called your office, and they told me that you were gone on vacation. I called your phone, but your number had changed. I was getting a little desperate I admit, so I came by your home. I just wanted to talk to someone. After I saw you with his wife, I was feeling a little left out. I know that I shouldn't have come by, but I didn't know what else to do. So, answer me truthfully, are you sleeping with his wife?"

"Why do you ask?"

"I saw her lying nude through the door."

"Well, since you must know, yes, I am," Kimberly told her.

"Is that why you wanted me to try to get Dr. Wilkes?

"Yes, I wanted Peyton for myself."

"Are you in love with her?" Kimberly felt no need to hide her love for Peyton; in fact, she was proud of their love. "Yes, I am."

"What you and I had, was that just pleasure, or do you think that you could've fallen in love with me?"

"Rebecca, you're a fabulous woman. What we had was fun and sexually fulfilling, but I could tell that you were looking for something else, and so was I. The plan was that you would end up with Gil and me with Peyton. At the end of the day, we all would end up okay. But it didn't happen that way."

"Yeah, but you're the only one who got what they wanted."

"Is it my fault that you didn't?" Kimberly asked.

"No, I guess not."

"You had the same opportunity that I had. You chose to act when you did. Don't blame me because your timing was off."

"I'm not blaming you."

"Yes, you are! You seem to be feeling resentment towards me because you didn't get what you wanted. You didn't listen to me. You chose to do things your way, and you fucked up. That's not my fault. You should've known not to try him at the clinic. His wife has a key to that clinic. That place is just like their home. She comes and goes as she pleases. She had the right to. She had no reason to believe that she would catch her husband in a compromising situation there. You were supposed to seduce him and get him to fall in love with you slowly. You acted hastily, now you're assed out, and you're blaming me. Now how am I supposed to help you if you are going to blame me?"

"I'm sorry."

"Are you going to get yourself together and let me try to help you, or do you want to take your chances on your own?" Kimberly was only saying this to keep tabs on Rebecca.

"Yes, I'm going to let you help me." Kimberly took her hand.

"Okay, now don't call me. I'll call you with plans for what we're going to do, but you're going to have to be patient."

"Okay. How long do you think it'll be before you call me?"

"Look, I don't know, but I'll be in touch." Rebecca hardly believed Kimberly, but she had no choice but to agree. Kimberly went into her purse, pulled out some cash, and dropped it on the table.

"I have to get back to the office. I'll be in touch. She got up from the table and left the restaurant. She called Peyton to check in with her. Everything was okay with her so she went back to the office. She was feeling a little uneasy with Rebecca. Rebecca was desperate, and this could cause trouble for her. Gil wanted Peyton back. There was nothing she could do as far as getting Gil to give Rebecca another chance. Rebecca acted as if she was unwilling to accept the truth. Kimberly tried to get some work done. She was worried all that day about what Rebecca might try. She decided to keep an eye on her for now. The only thing that even remotely brought her a sense of peace was that Peyton was home waiting for her. She thought it would be nice for the two of them to get out that night. They both needed to let their hair down.

She called Peyton to see if she would be up for a night out on the town. Kimberly went home, and she and Peyton began to get dressed for the evening. While they were in the Bahamas, Kimberly purchased a cute, sexy little dress for Peyton. The color was an eye-catching blood-orange. It was formfitting, and it fit Peyton's petite frame to perfection. She suggested that Peyton wear it for the evening. Peyton didn't know it, but Kimberly planned to take her to a nightclub she usually attends. This club, although very sophisticated, is a favorite for high-class lesbians. Kimberly knew that she probably wouldn't want to go if she told Peyton beforehand. So, she decided not to tell her. Once they were dressed, they left.

When they arrived, the valet driver took their car. A beautiful tall blonde met them at the door. She recognized Kimberly as one of the regulars. Kimberly was friends with the owner. She had represented her in a court case; they've been associates ever since. This club had no shortage of beautiful women, all of whom were lesbians. Most of the women who frequented this club were elite women in the community, mostly wealthy professionals. Kimberly was one of their big spenders, and they loved her at the club. They treated her like royalty when she came in. Normally, Kimberly would come alone. She brought Shawna, Dawn, and Rebecca a few times. Kimberly spoke to the woman at the door. She introduced Peyton to her. When the woman saw Peyton, she drew in a deep breath and eyed her, intending to flirt with her later. Kimberly noticed and pulled Peyton close signaling this date was personal and not just a fling.

"Would you like your regular table, or would you like something a little cozier?" Kimberly wanted Peyton to feel comfortable, so she took her to a private area of the club upstairs with semi-tinted windows with a view of the entire club. "I'll take a V.I.P. tonight, please," Kimberly responded. The young lady took them to their section upstairs. She asked Peyton what she would like to drink. Kimberly ordered vodka for them both. The hostess left the room. Peyton looked around the club. She noticed beautiful women everywhere. There were no men in the club. Exotic women were dancing and waiting on tables. Peyton thought they all looked like models. It was then that she realized that she was in a lesbian club.

"Do you come here often?"

"Yes, quite often. This is where I can come and be myself and let my hair down, no questions asked."

"Have you dated any of the girls here," she asked.

"I don't see any here that I have dated."

"They're all so beautiful," Peyton said.

"Yes, they are, but I don't just go for beauty," Peyton asks her,

"What's your type of girl?"

"I can't say that I actually have a type. It just depends on the woman."

"How long have you been interested in women?"

"I've been interested in them since I can remember. I've always been fond of women. Even when I was a young girl, I felt attracted to the same sex. I feel I was born this way. All I know is that although people judge me for my choice, I still love God, and I love his saints. People don't seem to care about that. They don't even try to understand me. They think because I'm lesbian, suddenly, I'm an enemy of God. Some of them seem to think He sweeps their sins under a rug. Anyway, I liked guys back then, but during college, I wanted to act on my feelings for women. My first experience with a woman was in our first year in college. I was invited to a party with ladies from another college. I met this beautiful woman named Brenda.

She was a twenty-three-year-old math major. We talked for a while, and we got to know each other better. I was interested, but mostly, I was curious. We made plans to go to Vegas for the weekend. We had sex, and I was hooked. She wanted a long-term relationship, but I was still interested in men then. She gave me an ultimatum: quit sleeping with men, or she would end our love affair. At that time, I was still trying to make a relationship between myself, and this guy happen. I never really had great experiences with men. Mom and Dad kept putting pressure on talking about marriage and grandchildren. Dad's looking forward to grandsons. I just wanted everybody to leave me alone and let me find my own way. After trying to make relationships work with men for a while, I quit dating them altogether. Most of the men that I dated were childish and full of games.

I never told you this, but one time while we were in high school, I went out with this guy. It was our first real date. I was so excited. Girl, he was everything I dreamed of. The night started off great, with dinner, movies, and bowling. Afterwards, he took me to a club that was owned by his family. The club was closed. We went inside, and we had a couple of drinks. We began to make out. He got up and turned out all the lights. The club was pitch black. I was totally nude. We continued making out when suddenly,

I began to feel hands other than *his* touching me. It had been a set-up. He had several of his friends there to try to sleep with me. He seriously thought that I was going to let that happen. When I refused them, he called me names and began yelling at me. His friends laughed and jeered at me. I was unable to see their faces through the darkness. After fighting them off, I fumbled for my clothes, and I demanded that he take me home. The club was a long way out on the outskirts of the city. I had never been on that side of town before, so I didn't quite know where we were.

He told me that if I slept with them, he would take me home. I cursed them all out and I left the building half-naked. There I was, walking alone in the back woods with no streetlights, or houses for miles. I saw several of them get in their vehicles and pass me by, laughing and throwing beer bottles at me. One of them had a bout of decency and followed me for about a mile as I walked along the roadside. He was trying to convince me to get in the car with him. He apologized for the group and took me home. I never told anyone because I was too embarrassed that I had allowed that to happen to me."

"I'm so sorry that you had to go through that alone," Peyton said. She took Kimberly by the hand.

"After that ordeal, I began to like women more. I can remember when I first met you in high school. I thought that you were so lovely. I didn't necessarily want to sleep with you at that time. I just liked you because you were kind to me. Can you remember? I was new to the school, and I had no friends. You were the first person who came to me. I guess all the other girls were too jealous or intimidated by me, but not you."

"I remember that," Peyton said smiling.

"All the boys wanted to know who you were. They thought that you were one of the hottest girls that they had ever seen, and you were right; most of the girls were jealous of you. You had the whole school going crazy."

"I thought of you as an angel. There you were, standing at your locker, smiling. You stood out among all the others because you had a smile that was so warm and inviting. I felt at ease as soon as I saw you. I knew then that I wanted to get to know you. I wanted to know what made a girl like you who was so beautiful, be so nice. My life changed after meeting you. You're the only person that's never judged or criticized me. You love me for who I am and you never, not even once, had anything negative to say about me. That's why I'm so crazy about you. You're the one who got me going to church. I was tough on the outside, but inwardly I wanted to be just like you. You were kind, feminine, and very sweet." Peyton smiled and said,

"Yeah, but Kimberly you had your own personality. You were beautiful, tough, and funny. You're very smart and a motivated hard worker. It wasn't your personality to be like me."

"I'm so grateful that you were always there for me. I knew by the time we were in college; I really began to warm up to you, wishing that we could be more than friends. I fantasized about you often. I was always afraid to approach you about it. Then you met Gil, and I knew I needed to start thinking realistically. I loved you so much, and I wanted to support you. All that mattered to me was your happiness. But believe it or not, I've always wanted your love, not only as a friend but as my lover. I love you, Peyton. I've been carrying this passion for you since college, and it's never gone away. With the passing of each day, my love for you has grown." Kimberly and Peyton were still holding hands at this point. Kimberly put her other hand over Peyton's hand.

"Promise me that you'll never leave me." Peyton looked at her with a bit of uncertainty.

"I'll never stop loving you," she said. "We'll always remain close." Although Peyton felt that she was in love with Kimberly, she knew she should begin to think about her future. She was wondering at that moment if she wanted to remain in a lesbian relationship, or if she wanted to move on with her life. She was having fun, and she didn't want to disappoint Kimberly. Besides, they were out to have a good time, and she had plenty of time to think about what she wanted later. Their hostess came back with the drinks. She placed their drinks on the table.

"If you need anything else, page me." She gave Kimberly a device that would summon her if needed. "Okay," Kimberly said. The hostess left. Peyton needed to use the restroom. Kimberly pointed her in the direction of the restrooms. Peyton left, and Kimberly took a sip of her drink. She casually looked around the club and when she looked up, she noticed a cute redhead stopping Peyton and handing her a card. Kimberly didn't like what she was seeing. She sprinted from the table and was over there in a flash. She interrupted the young lady while she was still talking to Peyton.

"The lady is with me," she said sharply.

The young lady had handed Pcyton her card, so Kimberly took it from Peyton and handed it back to her.

"She won't be needing this. Kimberly said.

"I'm sorry," the young lady apologized. "I just wanted to give her my card. I'm a photographer and she's a lovely lady. My camera would love her. I just thought..." Kimberly interrupted her before she could finish her sentence.

"You thought that you were leaving her alone. Now go." Kimberly walked Peyton to the restroom, and she refused to leave her side all evening. She noticed other women lustfully eyeing Peyton. She was jealous and very protective of her. Peyton was enjoying herself. They danced and drank and had a great time. Kimberly didn't drink as much. She wanted to keep a watchful eye out for anyone who tried to hit on Peyton. After they partied, Kimberly had the valet get her car, and they left. Peyton was a little drunk, so Kimberly grabbed her purse and helped her out of the vehicle.

They went inside where Peyton took off her heels and lay on the couch. She was feeling good but a little tired from dancing all night in heels.

"Wow, Kimberly, I had a wonderful time tonight. We've got to go back again."

"You really enjoyed yourself, huh? Kimberly asked while rubbing her feet.

"I sure did," Peyton said with a tipsy laugh. I haven't had a good time like that in a while."

"Yeah, well, I thought that I was going to have to fight a few of those bitches in there tonight. They were all over you." Kimberly started helping Peyton take off her dress.

"I can't let you go there alone; someone might try and take you from me and I won't have that." Peyton smiled.

"They were just being nice."

"No baby, they were hitting on you."

"Now, who would want me my scrawny behind? There were tons of gorgeous women there tonight. They could've had their pick of any of them. What could they possibly want with me?"

"That's for me to know and trust me; you were one of the hottest women in that place, and that beautiful dress and those hot heels that you were wearing, I thought I was going to have hurt somebody over you."

"You're so sweet, but I can hardly believe out of all those lovely women there, that anyone would pick me."

"Well I did, and I'd choose you over all the women in the world," Kimberly said. Kimberly sat on the sofa next to her.

"You asked me earlier, what was my type of woman. You're my type. Everything that I want in a woman, I have in you. You are it." They lounged on the sofa and watched TV.

Chapter Ten

THEY MEET

Kimberly had already gone to work by the time Peyton woke. She looked at the clock and it was around eight-thirty a.m. She was still tired and a little hungover from the night before. She was lying on the sofa when she began to think about Gil. She was missing him. She was missing her old life. She felt a sense of guilt for how she had allowed her life to go in the direction that it has. All the godly principles she once stood for, were now a thing of the past. She did enjoy her life before all this happened. She began to think that maybe she should've handled her situation a little better. She thought, *"Perhaps I should've prayed more. I should've gone to the pastor and at least gotten some advice from him on what I could've done"*. She got up and went into the bathroom and looked in the mirror at herself. She began to cry. While crying, thoughts of her and Gil kept popping in her head. She slid down to the floor and cried uncontrollably.

"What's happening to me? What have I done with my life? Please Holy Father help me!" A sudden sense of peace came over her and she sensed a voice deep inside her say,

"I am here to help you. I have been here all along."

It was a still small voice. It was a voice that she was familiar with. It was the voice of her comforter. God was speaking from within her. "Father," she cried, "I need your help. I've made such a mess of my life. I've chosen the wrong path. I feel so bad. Forgive me, Lord. Please guide me into your truth, your word, and your will for my life." The comforting voice within said,

"I will lead you and guide you. I will comfort you." It was then the feelings of guilt and shame went away. She got up and showered and went into the bedroom and got one of Kimberly's bibles. She read it for about two hours.

She missed the bible. Reading it always brought her peace. It was like an old friend. She began to smile while reading. She was so into it that when her cell phone beeped it startled her. She looked at it. It was one of the young girls from the church that she had mentored. She read the text. *"Mrs. Wilkes. I'm in trouble and I need you. It's an emergency. Can you please call me? It's important."* She called her back right away. The voice on the other end picked up and she was crying.

"Shalissa?"

"Hi Mrs. Wilkes, I'm downtown at the hotel on third street. I need you to come and pick me up."

"What are you doing down there?" she asked.

"I can't talk about it right now. It's an emergency; can you come and get me?"

"Yes, I'm on my way."

"Okay," she said. "I'll be at the south corner of the building."

Peyton got off the phone and put her clothes on and left for the hotel. Shalissa was sitting on the corner. The young girl jumped in the car with Peyton. She was still crying. Peyton saw police officers and an ambulance leaving the hotel.

"Shalissa, what's going on?"

"Mrs. Wilkes, promise me that you won't tell my parents, okay?"

"Shalissa, I can't promise you that baby. You've got to tell me what's going on. Police are everywhere and an ambulance just left. What happened? Are you okay?"

"Yes ma'am," she said while still crying.

"Now look, I can't help you if you don't talk to me." The young girl proceeded to tell her what happened.

"We were having a birthday party for my friend Taylor. She's turning sixteen today and we wanted to celebrate. Her boyfriend Mike got the room and liquor for us. He's twenty-one. We were partying and some of the crew were drinking, smoking blunts and taking pills. Taylor was getting high on weed, then she took some pills. We decided to go swimming. None of us knew that Taylor couldn't swim. We were in the water having fun when someone noticed Taylor at the bottom of the pool. She was unconscious. The paramedics were trying to resuscitate her. The police took her boyfriend to jail for proving the drugs and liquor. They questioned me and they told me to call my parents. I told them that my parents were out of town and you were my guardian until my parents came back. Can you talk to them for me so that they'll let me go without calling my parents?"

"Shalissa, a young girl is hurt, and you were here when it happened. I think that your parents would want to know about this. You can't keep this from them. I'm sorry baby, but I've got to call them."

"But Mrs. Wilkes, my parents are going to kill me when they find out that I lied! I told them that I was spending the night with my friend because we were doing a school project. That was the reason they allowed me to go."

"Baby, they have the right to know. Besides, you're a minor." Peyton called Shalissa's mom and told her everything, then took her over to where the police were standing. She introduced herself to them as a family friend and an attorney. One of the officers recognized her because she helped his grandmother during her time of need. "Mrs. Wilkes, I thought I recognized you. Do you remember me?"

"Refresh my memory," she said as he shook her hand.

"You helped my grandmother by donating the money when she was about to lose her home to the bank. They were getting ready to foreclose on her home, but you and your husband stepped in just in time and made the final payment."

"Are you referring to Mrs. Henrietta Patterson?"

"Yes, that's my grandma."

"I hope she's doing well."

"Thanks to you, she's doing amazing." After chatting with her for a few more minutes, he allowed her to sign for Shalissa. Her mother arrived, frightened and concerned. After Peyton told her everything the police officer shared with her, she took her daughter and left.

Peyton headed back to Kimberly's place. While on her way, she felt a strong urge to call Gil. She dialed the number, but she didn't press the call button. She was at a red light for what seemed like an eternity. She convinced herself to make the call. She did.

Gil answered on the first ring. She was still trying to figure out what she would say to him. She knew that they needed to talk. She felt that they needed to resolve the issues between them so they could move on with their lives. She was still confused. She loved Gil. She no longer hated or despised him. She was ready to try and deal with everything now. She was sober, and she didn't have Kimberly standing over her and influencing her.

"Hello Peyton," Gil said. Peyton was stumbling over her words.

"Hello Gil," she said.

"How are you?" he asked.

"I'm okay."

"Well, I'm glad to hear that." There was a brief silence, and then Gil said,

"I'm glad you called." Peyton didn't say anything. She was still trying to figure out what to say.

"Hello"

"I'm still here."

"I thought the call dropped."

"No, I'm here. Gil, I wanted to know if we could meet soon. I'd like to talk to you."

"Yes, we can," he replied.

"How soon would you like to meet?"

"How soon can you?"

"I'm not doing much now. Would you like to meet now?" Gil hoped she would say yes because he, too, was ready to resolve their issue.

"You don't have any surgeries scheduled for today?" she asked.

"No, I don't," Gil said. "I'm free."

"Okay, where can we meet?"

"Anywhere; you name it, and I'll be there."

"How soon can you be at the riverfront café?"

"In about twenty minutes," he said.

"Okay, well, I'll be there waiting for you." She got off the phone with him and drove over to the café. She was still sitting in her car when he pulled up. She saw him getting out of his vehicle and started walking over to hers. Her heart was racing, her throat was dry, and she felt sick to her stomach. She didn't know what she was going to say. He looked nice but a bit worn. His beard was a little scruffy, and he wasn't as clean-cut as usual. He walked over to her car and opened the door for her. She got out and thanked him.

"It's great to see you. How are you?"

"I'm doing okay."

"You look great.

"Thank you." They went inside and got a table. Gil was nervous but he was happy to see his wife. He didn't know what was going to happen that day, but he tried to stay calm. He thought he would lay low and allow Peyton to lead. They were seated. She didn't know where to begin. She drew in a deep breath and looked around the cafe.

"It's kind of busy around here today. Must be the lunch crowd, huh?"

"Yes, it's a little busy," Gil said. He looked at Peyton, studying her mood and facial expressions. Admiring her natural beauty, as she wasn't wearing any make-up, he smiled thinking of happier times. He missed her tremendously. He almost teared up thinking about her. Peyton turned her attention back towards him and noticed him lovingly gazing at her in awe. She remembered that look. She knew what it meant. She could tell he still loved her. She wasn't there for reconciliation; rather, she was there to resolve their issues so that they could move forward with their individual lives. She began to speak, but before she could get her words out, Gil said,

"Peyton, I'm so sorry for the way I hurt you. I was wrong for what I did, and I don't blame you for not forgiving me. I shouldn't have allowed this to happen."

She began to shift her body around in her seat as if what he was saying was making her uncomfortable.

"Peyton, please, hear me out," he said. She decided to listen to him.

"I know this will be hard for you to hear, but bear with me. I've already lost you, so please allow me to tell you everything."

"Go ahead," she said.

"I've never made it a practice of lying to you. I've always been faithful and loyal to our marriage. I love you with my whole heart. My main goal in life was to love and protect you and take care of you. I need you to trust me when I tell you what I'm about to say. When I hired Ms. Morgan, I had no desire for her. I never wanted her. I thought that she was a beautiful girl, but my interest in her was strictly professional. I thought that she was interested in working at the clinic. The night you came by it had been a long day. I was unusually tired and sleepy. I couldn't keep my eyes open. Apparently, she drugged my coffee. After I had drank the coffee, I became drowsy, so I went into my office and went to sleep. I was awakened by Ms. Morgan. She startled me, and she was already going down on me. When I realized what was happening, I began fighting her off, and then you walked in. I didn't have time to explain it because I was still trying to figure it out myself. She caught me completely off guard. I never saw it coming. It wasn't planned, at least not by me." Peyton believed him because that very thing happened to her during her first sexual encounter with Kimberly.

"Why didn't you stop her?"

"I tried," he said.

"It all happened so fast. Trust me, Peyton, I never wanted her. I loved you then, and I love you now. I'm sorry I hurt you." She believed him, but now, she was in her own predicament. She couldn't condemn him because she was in an adulterous, lesbian relationship, and unlike Gil, she was a willing participant.

"I've been praying for us baby. I miss you. I love you. My life has been miserable since you left. I don't want any other woman but you. I know that you probably don't want anything to do with me, and I don't blame you. I only wish that you could forgive me now. That's all I can hope for, and for you to not hate me. You needed to know the truth. You were my life and my world. You completed me. I'll never allow my love for you to diminish."

Peyton was overcome with emotion as she listened to him. She sprinted from the table and tried to run to the restroom. Gil stood to his feet and took her by the arm.

"Honey, please don't leave." He pulled her close to him right there in the restaurant, not caring who was looking. He held his wife, and she cried uncontrollably. The waiter came over to assist them. Gil jammed his right hand in his pocket and pulled out a wad of bills and gave them to the waiter. "We're okay," he said. He walked Peyton out of the restaurant and sat on an available bench. When Peyton was calm, he suggested they take his car down to the park on Riverside Drive. They sat next to a small tree overlooking the Mississippi. He held her there. At that moment, her feelings for him began to resurface. She relaxed in his arms and enjoyed the comfort of his being there. He gently rubbed her back. He didn't say much. He didn't want to ruin the tender moment.

Almost an hour had passed, and Peyton was still in his arms. Something was happening to them, but neither of them could explain it. A healing took place, a force stronger than them sealing a bond between them. The feelings of euphoria were over them. He looked down at her and said,

"I love you, my wife." He kissed her lips. She gave in to the kiss. She needed it. She had craved it. Everything that they felt for each other was expressed in this kiss. They missed each other, and it was evident at the moment. Nothing else mattered. Peyton looked up at her husband. He looked down at her and smiled. All the pain and suffering that he had gone through was dissolved in their kiss. Peyton's heart forgave him, but she had a big problem; Kimberly!!!

She tried getting up, but Gil held her closer.

"Don't leave yet," he said.

"I have to go. I have some things that I must attend to.

"Can't it wait for a few minutes, please?"

"I guess I can stay for a few more minutes," she said. She relaxed into his arms. Gil was getting anxious and thought he would ask her about their relationship.

"Peyton, what are we going to do about us?"

"Let's enjoy this," she said.

"I need some time to think."

"I understand," he replied.

He wanted to enjoy her, so that's what he did.

"I was expecting to meet with you today to discuss our financial situation, our accounts, and a possible legal separation until we could figure out what we needed to do next," she told him.

"I don't care about the money; I don't care about anything. Your happiness is all I care about. If I don't have you, I don't have anything because all of this without you is meaningless. I didn't touch anything of yours. This money is just as much yours as it is mine. You could've taken it all, and it wouldn't have mattered to me one bit. I want you back, baby. I'm miserable without you. Please give me another chance. I'll never hurt you like this again. Come back home, baby. I need you," Gil pleaded.

"You don't understand," she said as she lowered her head.

"Things have changed. I'm not the same woman that you fell in love with. I'm a different person." She began to get upset.

"What's wrong baby?" He asked, trying to comfort her.

"Nothing," she said. She pulled away from him, stood to her feet, and started walking slowly back towards the car.

"I can't stay. I have to go."

"He took her back to her car." She was holding her composure until she got to her car. Once there, he helped her in.

"Thank you."

"When will I see you again? he asked.

"I don't know. I'll call you." She tried to hurry and close her door. He motioned for her to let her window down. He leaned in, kissed her cheek, and said, "Soon, I hope."

She gave him a dry smile, started her vehicle, and drove away. Once she was down the road and out of his sight, she let the tears flow. She wanted Gil and her relationship with Kimberly could prove problematic. She was regretting her current situation. She didn't know that things were going to go so well between her and Gil. If she hadn't been involved with Kimberly, there was a strong possibility that she would've considered working on their marriage. She was torn. *"How could I go back to Gil after living like this? If he knew what I was involved in, he would not want me back. I can't tell him. What am I going to say? Honey, your wife is a lesbian, and I'm in a love affair with my best friend. He would think that she and I have been sleeping together all along. He would never understand that this just happened."*

She drove back to Kimberly's place. When she drove up, she saw that Kimberly was home a little earlier than usual. She got out of her car and went inside. Kimberly was upset and acting strangely.

"Where in the hell have you been?" she asked angrily.

"What do you mean?"

"What do I mean? I mean where have you been? I've been calling your ass all day on your cell phone and here at the house, but I couldn't reach you. What have you been doing the reason you couldn't answer my phone calls or return my messages?"

"Why are you acting this way?" Peyton asked.

"I've been worried about you all day. I haven't heard from you, and that's not like you."

"I got a text from Shalissa from the church. She's one of the girls that I was mentoring. She was in trouble. I had to go downtown to get her."

"What do you mean, in trouble?"

"She was supposed to be at one of her friend's houses spending the night, but they ended up at a hotel downtown.

They were using drugs and drinking, and her friend almost drowned in the pool. She was too afraid to call her parents, so she called me. I went to get her, and I called her parents for her. I waited there for her mom to pick her up." Kimberly calmed down a little, but by then, Peyton was a little concerned about her actions. She was showing rage and jealousy, and this frightened her.

"Why didn't you just call me to tell me what was happening?" Kimberly asked.

"During all the excitement, it never crossed my mind. I just figured I'd call you once I made it back." Kimberly was silent for a second.

"Okay, I'm sorry that I got so upset, but I was worried about you."

"Look, Kimberly, I know that since all this has happened with me and Gil, you've been very good to me. You've looked out for me, and taken good care of me, but I can still look out for myself. You shouldn't be *that* worried about me. I'm not a helpless child." Kimberly walked over to her and placed her arm around her. Peyton, feeling annoyed by the moment, recoiled. Kimberly, confused by her reaction, asked,

"What's the matter?"

"Nothing," she replied. Kimberly tried to hug her again. Peyton gently pulled away.

"Why won't you let me touch you?"

"No reason," Peyton replied, but Peyton did have a reason. She was still thinking about her encounter with her husband. It was Gil's arms that she desired, not Kimberly's.

"I'm a little tired from all the excitement today. I think I'll go and read for a while." Peyton tried walking out of the room, but before she could do so, Kimberly grabbed her by the arm and flung her around so that they were facing each other.

"I want to make love to you right now," Kimberly said, aggressively taking off Peyton's blouse.

"Not right now," Peyton said.

"Give me a little time. I just made it here. I would like to freshen up a little and catch my breath." Peyton pulled away and went to the bathroom. She locked the door and closed the lid to the toilet seat. She started praying. *"Lord, I need to get out of this relationship, and I need you to teach me how. I know what I'm doing is wrong, but I don't know how to let go. I love her, but I think I still love my husband.*

181

Can you please tell me what to do? I'm so confused right now." Peyton stayed in the bathroom until Kimberly came to the door. Kimberly tried to open the door, but it was locked.

"Peyton, why did you lock the door?" Peyton sprinted from the toilet seat and unlocked the door for her.

"What is going on with you today?"

"Nothing," she said.

"You sure are acting a little different all of a sudden."

"No, I'm not Kimberly; a girl almost lost her life. That's not something that I'm used to. All I am asking for is a little time to unwind."

"Okay," she said. Kimberly left and went to the living room. Peyton took a deep breath; she grabbed a towel and washed her face. While Peyton was still in the bathroom, Kimberly's phone rang. It was Rebecca calling her. Kimberly went outside to her car and answered the phone. Rebecca demanded that Kimberly meet her immediately. Kimberly agreed to meet with her. She went into the bathroom and told Peyton that she had to leave immediately. Peyton was relieved. She didn't ask her any questions. Kimberly left and went to Rebecca's house.

Chapter Eleven

SET UP

Rebecca came to the door partially nude. Kimberly, playing it cool went inside. Rebecca was drinking a cocktail.

"What was so important that I had to drop everything and come over?" Rebecca closed the door behind her.

"Calm down; I only wanted to talk to you. I need your help."

"What is it this time?" Kimberly asked.

"Would you like a drink?"

"No, I'd like to know why I'm here."

"I'll get to that in just a sec. You should let me fix you a little something to sip on." Rebecca walked away to the kitchen. On her way there, she took the lace top off her lingerie and let it fall to the floor. She was topless and had on red lace panties. Kimberly was a little turned on, but she wasn't impressed. She needed to know what she was up to. Rebecca fixed Kimberly a drink and gave it to her.

"Is this safe to drink?" Kimberly asked as she ran the drink underneath her nose for a quick whiff.

"Of course it is. Relax," she told her." Rebecca sat on her sofa, put her feet up, lay back, and sipped her drink. She batted her eyes at Kimberly in a flirtatious move. Kimberly was watching her closely, still trying to figure out what she was up to. Kimberly was looking at her shapely bronze legs and reminiscing about the great sex they had.

"I know you're wondering why you're here," she said as she took another sip of her drink.

"The truth is, if I had told you what I wanted, I knew that you probably wouldn't have come over."

"What makes you say that?" Kimberly asked while sipping her drink. Rebecca stared at Kimberly seductively. She placed her feet on the floor and moved her hips to the sofa's edge. She spread her legs, which excited Kimberly. Her mouth began to salivate, wanting to taste Rebecca.

"What is it that you want?" Kimberly asked.

"If I told you, would you give it to me?"

"I don't know; it depends on what that might be." Rebecca placed her hands between her legs and began entertaining her audience. Kimberly looked on intently; "Do you need help with that?"

"I could use a hand," Rebecca said as she continued to pleasure herself in Kimberly's presence. Kimberly moved closer to the sofa where Rebecca was sitting and joined her. They were kissing, and before long, they were having sex. They were at it for hours; what began on the sofa ended in the bedroom. Rebecca was very giving. Kimberly had been into pleasing Peyton so much that she had almost forgotten about her own sexual needs. It had been a while since she had sex with someone with this level of experience. It was three-thirty in the afternoon when Kimberly arrived at Rebecca's place. They had sex until about eight p.m. that night. Afterwards, Rebecca fixed them both another drink, and they lay there and talked.

"So, is this what you wanted?" Kimberly asked her.

"Yes, it is," she said. "I've never had anyone to make me feel like you do. I wanted to have fun one last time before we go our separate ways. I wanted to try and catch you before you got home because I knew that once you made it there, you wouldn't come out for anything. You are so caught up with your friend and all."

"Look, stay out of that now," she said, scolding her.

"I didn't mean anything by it; I was just saying." Rebecca quickly changed the subject. Rebecca told Kimberly that she was no longer interested in getting Gil. She told her that she was moving on with her life and that she had gotten over it. Kimberly was very intoxicated. Rebecca mentioned their scheme to break up the couple. Kimberly, feeling a little proud that her plan had worked, began to brag about it. After getting Kimberly to admit everything they had planned from the beginning, Rebecca asked for more sex. Kimberly obliged. This time, it was over quickly. Rebecca got up and showered. She told Kimberly that she had another engagement and that she had to leave soon. Kimberly knew that she had better be getting back home. She showered and put her clothes on. She thanked Rebecca for a great evening.

Kimberly was relieved to hear that Rebecca was no longer interested in Gil and that she wouldn't be pressuring her anymore about it. She also thought that she would keep her around for a little fun from time to time. Rebecca agreed to Kimberly's suggestion that they meet again.

After Kimberly left, Rebecca went to her entertainment center and turned off the hidden digital recorder. She checked in to see if she had gotten any footage. She went into her bedroom, got the other one, and checked it. She had strategically placed both cameras so that she could record everything.

"Great," she said. "I got it all." Gil was supposed to be Rebecca's ticket to a life of wealth and opportunity. Medical school was expensive, and she was already in a mountain of debt due to thousands of dollars in student loans. Since her plan didn't work, she wanted to make Kimberly pay them off. She also wanted to make her life just as miserable as hers. After all, she was her co-conspirator.

Peyton was lying in bed when Kimberly came home. She didn't know where she could've been all that time, and she didn't care all that much. She didn't feel like being romantically involved with her. All she wanted was to be left alone so she could have time to think. She pretended to be asleep. Kimberly, on the other hand, was exhausted. She didn't want to answer any questions that Peyton might have had so she came in quietly. Kimberly took another shower and went to bed. She slipped into the bed softly so as not to wake Peyton. When morning came, Kimberly went to work. She didn't talk to Peyton much. She was feeling a little guilty, but she was satisfied. On the other hand, Peyton got her a bible and began to read it again. She wanted to call Gil.

It turned out she didn't have to call him because he called her. She was glad he did. She let him do all the talking.

"Hi baby; are you doing okay today?"

"I am," she said.

"I was just sitting here reading."

"Oh yeah; what are you reading?"

"The Bible," she said.

"Yeah, that's always good reading. Any subject in particular that you're studying."

"No, I was just flipping through reading verses at random."

"Okay. I wanted to check on you to see how you were doing. You were a little upset yesterday when you left. I just wanted to make sure that you were alright."

"I'm alright. I just get emotional sometimes." Gil had never really seen her get emotional to that degree. She was always sweet yet strong. He thought that she may have been still upset because of the incident. He apologized to her again and tried to explain it to her again.

He talked and talked. By the time they were done talking, two hours had passed. By then, they were a little more comfortable with each other. They even shared a few laughs.

"So, what are your plans for today?"

"I have no real plans today. I was going to read a little more and then thumb through the phone book to look for me an apartment. I've been thinking a lot since yesterday. I need to move out of Kimberly's place and get my own. I've been here a little too long and need my own space."

"Why not just live in one of our condos?" he asked. Gil really wanted her to consider returning home, but he knew it was too soon for him to ask. If she hadn't gotten into a relationship with Kimberly, she probably would've moved into one of the condos.

"That's definitely something that I need to consider," she said. Actually, it was a great idea, but what would she tell Kimberly? Kimberly had this grand life planned for them, but Peyton no longer wanted that. Ever since she prayed that prayer in the bathroom, something inside her changed. Her vision was no longer cloudy. Things were much clearer. She wasn't the hopeless individual filled with turmoil and pain from a few months back. She needed a change.

"Why don't you consider it?" Gil said, speaking of the condo.

"I'll think about it." After a brief silence, Gil asked her, "What are you doing this Sunday?"

"I don't know. I had nothing planned. Why?"

"I was going to ask if you'd consider attending church with me."

"Church? she asked. I haven't been there in quite a while."

"I know, and everyone misses you, especially your girls. They ask about you all the time."

"You've been going to church?"

"Yes, I have; every Sunday and Wednesday night," he replied. "I have been so distraught over the events that have taken place in my life. I had to be in church. It was the only way that I could cope. I'd never planned on losing you. I prided myself on being a good husband and doing the right thing, then this woman came along, and without warning, she made sexual advances towards me in my sleep. I didn't want her. I wanted us. I was very happy in our marriage. My only problem then was that I felt that you were working too much. I never wanted to have an affair. I never initiated it. I know it looked bad, and believe me, if the tables were turned and I had walked in on something like that, then I would've only believed what I was seeing. I can honestly see why you were upset, but you must know that I didn't mean to hurt you. I miss you, honey. I'd love to see you again. Perhaps we can go to church and see where it goes. No pressure."

"I guess I can go," she said.

"Great, am I picking you up, or will you meet me there?"

"I'll meet you there," she replied. They talked until Peyton's phone beeped. It was Kimberly calling.

"I have another caller on the other line," she told him."

"Okay, can I call you a little later on?"

"I will call you tomorrow," she told him.

"Okay, I will be waiting." She answered her other line. "Hello,"

"Hey there," Kimberly said.

"What are you up to?" Kimberly asked.

"Nothing," Peyton replied in a friendly tone hoping that she wouldn't let on in her voice that something was up with her.

"What are you doing?"

"I was just sitting here reading."

"Are you doing okay?"

"Yes, I'm fine. Are you working hard?" Peyton asked.

"No harder than usual," Kimberly said. "I was just calling to check on you. I wanted to let you know that I will be taking you out to dinner tonight so please be ready."

"I was kind of thinking about staying in this evening and maybe cooking for us tonight," Peyton said.

"That sounds even better. Yeah, let's do that. I should be home around six. I'll call you and let you know when I'm on my way."

"What would you like for me to cook tonight?"

"I don't care," Kimberly said. "As long as you are there, I could eat anything. Well, I have to get back in here.

I'll call you when I'm on my way. I love you," Kimberly said while getting off the phone. Peyton recited her lines as well not feeling in love with Kimberly anymore.

"Me too."

Peyton got off the phone and went into the kitchen to see what they had there to eat. Kimberly hardly ever cooked. She ate out a lot, so she didn't keep anything to eat or cook in her fridge. Peyton looked inside but she couldn't scratch up enough food for a decent meal.

She saw that she had to go to the store, so she left for the marketplace. On her way there, Gil called her.

"Hello"

"Hi, I'm sorry to bother you, but I forgot to ask, are we going to the eight o'clock service or the ten o'clock service." Peyton smiled to herself,

"Let's make it ten o'clock."

"Okay, and lunch afterward?"

"I don't know, we'll see."

"Okay," he said, "I'll let you go." Peyton got everything for dinner and headed back to the house. While putting the food away, she thought about telling Kimberly that she would probably be moving out of her home. She was unsure if she was ready to move home with Gil or if that was even a good idea at this time, but she definitely needed to move out of Kimberly's place. *"Kimberly won't like it,"* she thought, *"But I have to get out of here and think."* Peyton prepared dinner and got dressed. Kimberly came home.

"Something sure smells good," she said out loud. Peyton smiled. Kimberly walked over and kissed her. Peyton turned her cheek so that Kimberly wouldn't kiss her on the lips.

"I can see it's you," Kimberly said. Peyton rushed past her. She pretended to be in a hurry to the kitchen to check on dinner. She didn't want to deal with Kimberly's unwanted advances. She went into the kitchen, got the food, and took it to the table. Kimberly freshened up and went to the dining area where Peyton was waiting on her. Peyton fixed Kimberly her drink. She opted out of drinking. She sipped apple juice instead.

"I'm looking forward to making love to you tonight," Kimberly told her.

"I need a good hot bath and want nothing else but you this evening."

"I'm sorry, baby, but I think we are going to have to wait. It's that time of the month for me," Peyton said, surprised at how quickly she came up with that excuse.

"Oh no," Kimberly said.

"I wish I had known. I was so looking forward to loving you tonight."

"I know," Peyton said, trying to sound disappointed but glad that she had bought herself some time.

"I'm sorry."

"No need for apologies," Kimberly said.

"At least I can hold you tonight." Peyton cleared her throat. She was ready to tell Kimberly she wanted to move out.

"Baby," Peyton said softly to Kimberly.

"Yes, what is it?"

"I've been doing a lot of thinking. When I first came here, I was only going to be here temporarily. I had no plans on staying long-term. I'm feeling a lot better, and I think it's time for me to move into my own place." Kimberly was visibly upset.

"What do you mean, get your own place? This is your home. You live here with me. You're my woman. I don't want you to leave."

"I know, but I need my own space. I've already made up my mind. This is something I need to do. I'm not breaking up with you or anything like that. I just need some time to get my life together. I've got to find out who I am and what I want to do with my life. I've lived my life for others, and now it's time for me to live my life for myself. I appreciate all that you've done for me. But If I'm going to keep my sanity, then I'm going to have to find myself. I've been doing a lot of praying and reading my bible and soul searching."

"Are you regretting our love," Kimberly asked.

"I don't know. I think that deep down in my heart, I know what I'm doing is wrong, but I've never confronted the issue. I just got a little caught up in the passion of all of it. It was new to me, and I enjoyed it for a while. Now I think it's time that I start thinking about getting my life back on track, and the start to that is getting my own place."

"You're just emotional because it is your time of the month. Give it a couple of days and you'll come around."

"No Kimberly, It's not that. I must do this. If you truly love me as you say you do, then you'll let me do this."

"I want to let you know that I'm not going to let you leave me. You're mine, and I love you. You can get your own place for now, but you're still my girl, and don't you forget that."

"I understand," Peyton said. She didn't feel like arguing with her. She only wanted to make it very clear to her that she would be moving out. Kimberly could tell that Peyton had changed in the last couple of days, but she thought nothing of it. "So, when are you planning on moving out?"

"I was thinking perhaps this month." Peyton was thinking more along the lines of the next day, but she didn't want to hear Kimberly's mouth.

"Okay well, you have my blessing." Kimberly was a master manipulator. She agreed with Peyton because she was sure of her ability to manipulate her into coming back. If she tried to stop her at that point, then she would definitely lose her. After dinner, they went into the bedroom, where Kimberly held her for a while. Kimberly began trying to manipulate her, but Peyton was much stronger this time, and she hadn't been drinking, nor had she taken any of the sedatives that Kimberly would feed her. As Kimberly held her close, all Peyton could think about was Gil's apology. She missed him and she wanted to open a line of communication with him. Kimberly had painted him out to be an awful monster, but Peyton actually knew him, and she didn't see that in him, especially now that she had learned the truth. Peyton went to sleep thinking about Gil.

Chapter Twelve

BLACKMAIL

Kimberly got out of bed, got dressed, and went to the nightclub for a drink and to clear her head. There were a lot of beautiful women there and it would've been easy for her to pick one up and take her to a hotel room, but she wasn't feeling that. She was wondering if she was losing Peyton. She would stop at nothing to keep her in her life. She thought, *"What could've happened in the last couple of days that caused her to have a drastic change of heart?"* She didn't know but she was about to go into overtime to find out. She got drunk fast. She was ordering drinks one after the other. She had to come up with a plan. She got her keys and left the club.

While on her way home, she just happened to notice Rebecca at a convenience store. She pulled her car alongside Rebecca's car. She was coming outside the store when she pulled up. Kimberly let down her window and called her name. Rebecca looked startled but when she recognized Kimberly, she went to her window. They chatted for a few minutes. Kimberly flirted with her and Rebecca flirted back. Rebecca knew this was another opportunity to continue to get Kimberly to further incriminate herself. She asked Kimberly to come home with her. Once there, Rebecca set the mood with fragrant candles, and she gave Kimberly more to drink. Kimberly went to use the restroom and while there, Rebecca set up the camera in her bedroom. When Kimberly came out of the bathroom, Rebecca was already undressed. Kimberly went stumbling through Rebecca's apartment looking for her. She called out to her.

"Hey girl, where are you?"

"I'm in here," Rebecca said. Kimberly went into her bedroom.

"Damn girl," she said looking at Rebecca in her lingerie.

"You're fine as hell." Kimberly fell onto Rebecca's bed drunk. Rebecca wasted no time. She climbed on top of Kimberly and began doing any and everything she could to quickly get her turned on, which wasn't difficult. Kimberly had no idea what she was up to. She felt that she had her under *her* control. Rebecca was desperate and she needed all the ammo she could get on Kimberly. Kimberly was very conniving, and she always got what she wanted. It didn't matter who got hurt in the process, so her time was due to come. Rebecca felt used by Kimberly and she threw her away like a piece of trash. Then to add insult to injury, she slept with her and was about to do so again. Rebecca couldn't let this happen to her this way. Her revenge would be sweet. What she wasn't aware of was that she was playing in the major league. Kimberly was a professional and had played this game and she always won. Kimberly would fight just for the sake of fighting, even if she didn't want what she was fighting for. She would be that much more eager to fight tooth and nail for something that she truly wanted. It was the dogmatic, fierce instincts that made her a great attorney.

Rebecca continued her performance for the camera. After they were done having sex, Kimberly went to sleep. Rebecca got up and got a camera and took pictures of Kimberly lying in her bed nude. Afterward, she put her clothes on and went through Kimberly's purse, found her cell phone, and copied every phone number on it. She found Peyton's number and she wrote it down. This is the number that she wanted.

If Kimberly didn't comply with her demands, then she would expose her to Peyton. She was also going to send Gil a letter telling him everything. She already made a recording of them having sex and discussing Kimberly's plan to get Peyton from Gil. Now she had even more ammunition. She could hardly believe her luck. She looked at Kimberly lying there in the bed nude. She resented her. She smirked as she watched Kimberly sleep.

"Sleep on you dirty bitch," she said under her breath.

"This will teach you to mess over me," she said as she took more pictures of her. After she had gotten all the pictures she needed, she put away her cameras, went into the living room, and lay on the sofa until morning.

The following day…….

Kimberly woke with a major headache. She had gotten so drunk, that she could hardly remember anything that happened after she left the club. She did remember going to Rebecca's place but anything after that was totally blank. She looked down at herself and noticed that she was nude and uncovered. She looked around the room and she wondered what time it was. She immediately jumped out of bed hoping that she had enough time to go home to Peyton. She had no intentions of spending the night with Rebecca.

She had intentions of going home and sleeping in her own bed with Peyton by her side. She was going to use this day to try and convince her to change her mind about moving out. That plan was spoiled now, and she was uncertain about how she was going to explain her absence to Peyton. She found her clothes lying at the foot of the bed. She grabbed them and put them on. She called out to Rebecca, but she got no answer. She didn't bother waiting for an answer. She grabbed her purse and headed out of the apartment. She looked in the mirror. "Damn, I look a mess," she said. Her hair was tangled all over her head. She tried to fix it with her fingers. She called Peyton but got no answer. This was cause for concern. She called the house number. She assumed that Peyton had already left. It was around seven-thirty a.m.

"Where could she be this early in the morning?" She headed to her place speeding all the way. She noticed that Peyton's car was still in the driveway, and she also noticed another car. It was Rebecca's!

"What in the hell is this bitch doing at my place?" she said out loud. She pulled up quickly and noticed that Rebecca was sitting in her car. She went up to her driver's side window. She knocked and motioned for her to let the window down. Rebecca looked up at her and smiled. She let the window down; Kimberly reached inside the window and grabbed her by her hair.

"Look bitch, I want to know what kind of game it is that you're playing here. What in the hell are you doing here at my home you fucking slut?" Rebecca looked at Kimberly with a wolfish grin and said,

"If you know what's good for you, then you would take your fucking hands off me. I've got your slut right here." Kimberly noticed a flash drive in Rebecca's hand and an envelope with what seemed to be photographs. She handed Kimberly the drive and the envelope. Kimberly slowly pulled her right hand out of Rebecca's hair.

"What is this?"

"Take a look, movie star," Rebecca said. Kimberly snatched the envelope open and saw the images of her and Rebecca engaged in sex, and some of her nudes of her lying in Rebecca's bed passed out drunk. She then looked at the flash drive in her hand, and Rebecca said,

"That's your very own porno movie, baby, starring you and me! Now, what do you know about that?" She threw her head back and laughed. Kimberly was furious.

"What in the hell do you plan on doing with these?" she asked.

"Nothing if you do what I ask. Now those are yours, a little gift from me to you. I've got to go now. I'll be in touch," she said to Kimberly. She let her window up, and she winked at Kimberly, and then she blew her a kiss. Kimberly was speechless. She couldn't believe that Rebecca had done this. She put everything in her purse, and she went inside. When she got in the door, she saw that Peyton was asleep. Her morning was ruined. Peyton was leaving, Rebecca was threatening her, and her timing couldn't be worse. She climbed into the bed with Peyton.

Her heart sank at the thought of losing her. Tears formed in her eyes. For the first time in a long time, she was afraid. She wasn't in control. She was backed into a corner and didn't know what to do. Her only option was to play it by ear. Peyton began moving around in the bed. She had slept so soundly that she didn't notice Kimberly hadn't come home until morning. She opened her eyes. Kimberly was lying there watching her.

"Good morning," Peyton said.

"Good morning," Kimberly said to her with tears still in her eyes.

"Is everything okay? You look like you've been crying, are you upset about something?"

"No, not really," she said.

Peyton sat up in bed and looked at Kimberly. She had never seen her look so pathetic and vulnerable before in her life.

"Come on, Kimberly, tell me what's wrong." Kimberly looked at her.

"Well, for starters, you're leaving. I love you, and I hate to see you go. My mind can't fathom the thought of losing you, and it's painful. It's like you're deserting me. When you needed me the most, I was there for you, and now it seems like you're running out on me. When Gil slept with that woman, I was there for you. I was there when he turned his back on you and betrayed you. When you needed a friend and a shoulder to cry on, I was there, and now you're abandoning me. I love you, Peyton, and I don't want you to go."

"Look, Kimberly. I care about you, too. I thank you for everything that you've done for me, and I mean that. I appreciate you, but now it's time for me to do what I feel is best for me. I need to take some time to get my head together and see what I will do about my life. I need to start looking out for myself and my own needs. I've had a lot of people who looked up to me and who needed me, and I just checked out on them, and I let them down. I have to get my prioritics straight." Kimberly saw that her mind was already made up and said,

"You're right baby; I guess I'm being a little selfish. You take all the time you need. You have that right." Peyton reached for her hand.

"I thank you for understanding," Peyton said.

Chapter Thirteen

THE MOVE

Peyton got dressed after Kimberly left. She drove to a home that she and Gil owned. It was a four-bedroom, two-and-a-half-bath home on a five-acre spread just on the outskirts of town. The grounds were immaculate and there was a large man-made lake. They also had several horses on the property, and it had a small horse trail where they went riding. It was peaceful. The couple would come here when they were trying to get away from everyone. No one knew that they owned this piece of property, not even their parents. It had been almost a year since they had been there.

Peyton took in a deep breath as she drove up to the property. She felt all of her troubles rolling away. She went inside and looked around. She knew this was the perfect place for her to clear her head and begin to work on getting her life back on track. She called up the staff and security to let them know that she would be staying there indefinitely and that they needed to get everything in order. She went back to Kimberly's place and gathered all of her belongings that she was taking with her. She took the blood-orange evening dress that Kimberly purchased and laid it on the bed. She wrote a goodbye note and laid it on top of the dress, signaling that that chapter of her life was now over. She left for her new home. After she got settled in, she followed up with a phone call to Kimberly. There was no answer, so she left her a message. After she was comfortable, she made a list of things that she needed and gave it to Jan, one of the staff members, to go out and purchase. She went outdoors and walked out towards the lake. She stood on the dock and drew in a deep breath. When she exhaled, she felt peace. She admired the mid-morning sun as its rays danced on the water, giving off a shimmering effect. Seeing the ducks waddling along in a row, tending to their young, and the lovely flowers at the lake's edge, made her breathe a sigh of relief. She was free. Nobody was breathing down her neck and telling her what to think or how to feel. Her senses were returning in this short time, and she felt like she was being reborn.

She didn't want anyone, not Gil or her parents, to know where she was for now. She would call them in a few days, but she took this time for herself.

Kimberly had been in court all day. It was around three o'clock when she finally got a break. She headed back to her office. While on the way, she checked her messages. When she got the message from Peyton, her heart stopped. She didn't know that she was leaving so soon. She made a U-turn in the middle of Poplar Street and made her way to the expressway. She hurried home to see if it was real. When she arrived, she saw that all of Peyton's things were gone. She found the note, the dress, and her door key. The note read, *"Kimberly, I love you and thank you for everything. I'm going through some things emotionally and spiritually, and I need to deal with them. I thank you for allowing me this time to gather my thoughts. I thank you for understanding. Love Peyton"*

Kimberly felt sick. She had pulled out all the stops in trying to get Peyton. She began plotting again. She had to try to win her back, but there were a few obstacles. The first thing she needed was to handle the issue with Rebecca.

She began by calling her to see what her reasoning was behind the blackmail. Rebecca immediately answered.

"I see that you are ready to talk business," Rebecca said to her.

"What do you want?" Kimberly asked

"I'll tell you that later," Rebecca said with confidence, feeling that she was holding all the cards.

"What do you mean by later?" Kimberly asked in a nasty tone.

"I'll call you later and then I will explain more, but right now, I have to go." Rebecca ended the call. Kimberly threw her phone across the bed in anger.

"That dirty bitch. I'll teach her who to play with."

She jumped up from her bed and went to her safe. She opened the combination lock. There she kept her business documents, wills, land leases, and a large sum of cash. Also, inside were her best jewels and two handguns. One was a revolver given to her by a former classmate turned big-time drug lord. It was a thirty-eight snub nose revolver. It wasn't registered and the serial numbers had been filed off. He had given her the gun after she was harassed in a rough part of town where they were in for a party. She never got rid of it. The other one, a nine-millimeter for ladies was registered to her. She closed the safe and got her purse. She wrapped the gun in a small scarf and placed it in her purse. She tried to call Peyton but when Peyton saw it was Kimberly, she refused to answer. Kimberly had the propensity to be very pushy, and she just wanted to be left alone. Peyton's not answering made Kimberly even more upset. Kimberly had been so sure of herself, and she thought that she had Peyton in the palm of her hand. Furthermore, she had underestimated Rebecca. This infuriated her because she didn't see it coming. She prided herself on being able to manipulate people and situations to benefit her and now the game was being turned on her. This challenged her.

With Peyton gone, she's ready to play hardball with Rebecca. She just needed to be patient. Kimberly was feeling like a warrior, and she was ready for battle. She would choose her strategy carefully. She couldn't win by losing her head. She bottled her feelings for Peyton temporarily in order to gain more strength for the battle. She was lying across her bed on her back when her phone rang. It was Rebecca. She was demanding that Kimberly meet with her, and it had to be right away and in a very public place. They agreed upon Audubon Park. Once there, they both got out of their vehicles and met up at a picnic table. It was around six o'clock in the evening. Rebecca looked at Kimberly with a sly smirk and said,

"Well, hello my lovely co-star." Kimberly was annoyed at her arrogance.

"What the fuck is all of this about you filthy cunt?" Rebecca placed her hands on her hips and looked at Kimberly, and said,

"Now I wouldn't resort to name-calling, my dear," she said smiling. I thought you were more mature than that. Have a seat, and we can talk like two mature adults."

Kimberly was seated. She was trying to control her anger, but she was boiling inside. Rebecca brought her laptop with her. She sat it on the table, opened it, and turned it on. Kimberly just watched and waited. Rebecca went into her email account and flipped the computer around to Kimberly. Kimberly noticed that Rebecca had the email addresses of her friends, partners at the firm, and most of her clients. She had everybody that was anybody's information, from professionals down to the hired help; she even had her parents' information. She had everyone's email addresses and phone numbers.

"How in the hell did you get all of this?"

"Don't worry about that. It doesn't matter how," she said. She started the video of her and Kimberly. She watched it taunting Kimberly with remarks that angered her even more.

"Damn girl, look at you." Rebecca turned her head sideways.

"Ooh, that felt so good when you did that. I almost lost my mind. I can see why Peyton left her hubby for you." Kimberly couldn't take any more. She jumped up and started walking towards her car. Rebecca yelled out,

"All I have to do is press send, and all of your acquaintances and business contacts will see your movie. Everyone will know about your evil ass, and you'll lose everything, and that position of power that you love lording over *us little ones* will be gone."

"Bitch, fuck you and those clients. I don't give a damn about this bullshit you're trying to pull. I'm rich!"

"Yeah, about that, since you are so *rich*, I would like to share in your good fortune. Now, you may not care about your clients or your reputation, but your sweet little woman Mrs. Wilkes. You will lose her. Is that what you want?"

Kimberly thought for a second. She knew that she would give up all of her cash to keep Peyton in her life. She turned back and looked at Rebecca.

"What do you want?"

"Oh, I can see that got your attention. There *is* *something* that you care about. She must have some sweet-tasting goodies."

"Look, you stay out of that," Kimberly snapped.

"Oh, how cute. You're in love. I'm so jealous." Rebecca laughed. 'I don't want much. All I want is for you to pay my way through medical school. I'm talking tuition, books; all equipment needed, from my room and board down to my ink pens. Oh, and eight-hundred-thousand dollars in cash. Since you're so *"Rich,"* that's got to be chump change for you."

"Bitch, you must be out of your damn mind. Now, where am I going to get that kind of cash? All of my money is tied up in stocks, bonds, and CDs. It only looks good on paper. At the most, I could come up with, what, eighty-thousand dollars? I can have that to you in the morning."

"No, no, no. I know better than that. You had better make something happen or else," Rebecca argued.

"Look, it's going to take some time for me to come up with that much cash."

"Okay, I'm going to work with you. I want the eighty thousand that you said you could have by morning, and I'm going to give you three days to come up with the rest. I've got to go. I have another meeting to attend."

"What, another blackmail meeting?" Kimberly asked sarcastically. Rebecca turned her laptop off and put it back in its case. She ignored Kimberly's comment. She started towards her car.

"I'll be in touch." Rebecca got in her car and left. Kimberly sat on the bench, plotting her next move.

"This bitch is pretty good, but I will have the last word." Kimberly got in her car and went home. She went to her safe and counted the money that she had inside. There was little more than eighty thousand inside. She took it out and put it in one of her bigger purses. She then took the pistol out of her purse and put it in the bag with the money. She got her phone and tried to call Peyton again. She got no answer. She didn't have much of an appetite, so

she got herself a glass of vodka, took a sedative, and went to bed.

In the meantime, Peyton was getting settled into her environment. She was enjoying herself. The peace and the beauty were what she needed, and it provided a tranquil place for her to get her head together. She was watching T.V. for a while and the phone to the residence rang. *"Now who in the world could be calling here this late in the evening? Nobody knows I'm here."* She answered supposing that it was the wrong number or possibly one of the staff members. It was Gil.

"Hello"

"Hi Peyton"

"Gil?"

"Yes, it's me."

"How did you know I was here?" she asked curiously.

"Jan called and asked if we were going to need anything else that wasn't on the shopping list. She said that she couldn't reach you by phone, so she called me. I tried your cell also and didn't get an answer."

"Oh, I walked out back by the lake," she said. Peyton forgot to tell the staff that she didn't want anyone to bother her there.

"I see you decided to take my advice and stay in one of the properties huh?"

"Yeah," she said, breathing out deeply. She was kind of disappointed that Gil knew where she was. She knew that he would probably try to call her, and she wasn't ready to do a lot of talking. She wanted to take this time to pray and heal.

"Are you okay? Do you need anything?"

"I'm fine. I have everything I need. I gave Jan a detailed list. The rest of the staff will be here tomorrow to get everything else ready for my stay. It'll probably take them a couple of days to get everything together and then only Jan and Thomas will be around.

Thomas was another one of their employees in charge of maintenance of the grounds and the upkeep of the vehicles and the boat. He was also in charge of the staff who took care of the horses. There's a small duplex cottage on the other side of the property which he and Jan reside when the Wilkes are on the property. Thomas lives there permanently. Jan's only there when the Wilkes' are there. She lives at the Wilke's estate which is their main property.

"Okay, well I'm glad that you decided to stay." There was this long awkward silence.

"Well, I'd better be going," Gil said.

"Okay," Peyton said.

"If you need me, call me, okay?"

"Alright." They said their goodbyes and ended the call. Peyton knew this wouldn't be the last of their conversation tonight. He was sure to call her back. Sure enough, about twenty minutes later he called back. Clearing his throat, he said,

"Um, I was just calling to see if we were still on for church this Sunday."

"Yes, we're still on for church this Sunday." She thought it was cute, but she knew that she couldn't rush into anything with him right then.

"I will meet you Sunday for the ten o'clock service."

"Okay," he said in a cheerful voice.

"Bye"

"I don't know what I'm going to do about that man," she said to herself. "I know he's not going to leave me alone." She looked over the fireplace mantle and noticed the photograph of her and Gil. She smiled, got up, and went into the kitchen. She got a glass of water, went back into the den, and turned on the television. She watched a little Christian television. There was a local pastor on TV with his wife and they were talking about forgiveness in marriages. Everything that Peyton needed to hear was on Christian television that day. Even the subject of forgiving yourself was discussed.

Peyton knew all of this. In the past, she was always doing her best to make the right choices. She practiced living a devout Christian lifestyle, but she never really practiced doing so-called sinful things. After watching television, she got her Bible and read it until Jan got there.

"I got everything you requested, Mrs. Wilkes," Jan said.

"I tried calling you to see if there was anything else you may have wanted, but I couldn't reach you. I called Mr. Wilkes. He said he would get you to call me, but I guess he forgot."

"You're okay, Jan. I didn't need anything else. Where is Thomas?"

"He's out back getting the rest of the things out of the trunk and parking the car."

"When you're finished putting everything away, I would like a small Caesar salad and a bottle of water."

"Okay, Mrs. Wilkes." Peyton went back into the den area. After eating, she went to bed.

Chapter Fourteen

IN FOR THE KILL

It was Friday morning. Peyton woke to the sun shining and the birds chirping. The smell of freshly brewed coffee was in the air. She sat up in bed. It was a beautiful day, and she was in good spirits. She called Jan, who was in the kitchen preparing breakfast. Jan came in. "I'll eat my breakfast out back on the sundeck, okay"

"Yes ma'am." Peyton got up and showered. She put on her robe and went out back. On her way there, she noticed an assortment of flowers, roses, and balloons all over the living room. Jan walked in while she was looking at them.

"Mr. Wilkes brought them by and left," she said.

"He sure is a sweet man. You two are so blessed to have each other," Jan said.

"How many years have you two been married?"

"Going on seventeen years," Peyton said.

"Wow, it must be nice to have your husband still that much in love with you after seventeen years of marriage. You guys keep up the good work. Your breakfast is ready ma'am. Will Mr. Wilkes be back? Should I prepare a little something for him?"

"No, that won't be necessary. Mr. Wilkes will not be here. Thank you, Jan. I'll call you if I need you."

"Okay," Jan said, going back into the kitchen to finish her duties. Peyton read the note on the card.

"Hello my wife. I do hope you are getting settled in just fine. I wanted to brighten your day. I'm looking forward to seeing you on Sunday. Gil" She almost wished that she had gotten to see him when he brought them by. She got the phone and called him. He answered.

"Thank you, Gil," she said. His heart was filled with joy because she called. "Anything for you beautiful. Have a wonderful day"

"You too," she said. She didn't want to end the call, but she did. She sat for a minute, just holding the card. She had almost forgotten about her breakfast until Jan came in and asked her if she had changed her mind. After breakfast, she took a walk down by the lake. She sat there and she seriously thought about the possibility of getting back with Gil. She felt that even if they did get back together, she would have to tell him the truth about her and Kimberly, which frightened her. She didn't think that he would take the news well. It weighed on her so heavily that she felt a little tension.

She decided to enjoy her day and not worry about anything. She had the staff saddle her horse and rode off any tension she felt. Looking on the bright side, since moving, she was happier and less stressed. She was also on speaking terms with Gil, which was a good thing. At one point, she couldn't even think about him without breaking down. Life was getting better for her. She chose to take life one day at a time.

Kimberly was up and dressed for the office. Her day was not so beautiful. She'd awakened to an empty bed. Her life was spiraling out of control. She went to the bank and withdrew twenty thousand dollars. She put it in the bag with the rest of the money. She drove over to her office and waited for Rebecca's call. She had to be in court a little later that day. Finally, her cell phone rang. It was Rebecca. Kimberly knew that she wouldn't gain anything by losing her cool. She began her conversation by being overly friendly to Rebecca. She said, "Hey girl. I have your money, but I have court today; I can meet with you later. You name the time and place, and I'll be there."

"Okay, but you better show up if you know what's good for you."

"I understand," she said. Kimberly remained cool and calm even though she wanted to curse at her. They ended their call.

Kimberly handled her business. She went to court, and she had a very successful day in court. She tried calling Peyton again, but there was no response. After she was done, she drove home. She called Rebecca to meet. Again, she was overly friendly. She was acting like a helpless victim. Rebecca didn't know what to think about Kimberly's behavior. *"Why is she being so nice? Just downright wimpy,"* she thought...*almost pathetic."* After talking with her, she felt sorry for her. She let her guard down, and they met at a restaurant. Kimberly passed her the money. Rebecca almost felt a little guilty taking it. She was caught off guard by Kimberly's bazaar behavior.

"Thank you," she said as she took the money.

"No problem," Kimberly said.

"Who cares about money anyway? It doesn't mean a damn thing to me. You work hard all your life to get this shit, and, in the end, it doesn't deliver what you think it will. It only matters to the people who don't have much of it. It can't solve relationship problems. When you are hurting, it does nothing for you. I have all this money but what for? I don't care about it. You can have it all. I even put an extra twenty thousand in there for you. I want to apologize for all the pain and hurt that I caused you. I know you must think I'm some monster, but I'm not."

She went on and on about all the bad things that happened to her in her life. She seemed suicidal. Rebecca began to feel sorry for her. They left the restaurant. Rebecca offered for her to come back to her place. Kimberly went with her, and they talked and talked. At one point, Kimberly began to cry on Rebecca's shoulder. Rebecca got her some tissues. She handed them to Kimberly, and she sat beside her. Rebecca put her arm around Kimberly's shoulder and began to comfort her. Kimberly kissed her. The next moment, they were having sex. Kimberly was extremely passionate and caring. She treated Rebecca as though she was in love with her. Rebecca had not seen this side of her.

Rebecca almost felt guilty about what she was doing to Kimberly. When they were finished, Kimberly continued to tell her sad stories.

"Most people just misunderstand me," she said. "I always had to do more to get more she said. I'm not all that bad; it's just my way of protecting myself from people so that I won't get hurt. People are so mean and dirty to each other, and they are always out to get one another."

Rebecca felt awful by the time Kimberly was done talking. She began apologizing and explained her actions of the blackmail to her. Kimberly said,

"There's no need to apologize. I guess you did what you felt you needed to do. It's only natural." Rebecca got up and went to get her laptop. She went to her closet and got a briefcase with the original flash drive. She sat by Kimberly and handed her the briefcase. In it were the extra copies of movies that she had made to distribute if Kimberly refused to pay.

"I'm so sorry for the way I treated you. I was hurting inside, and I acted out in this way toward you. It was selfish of me to blame you for my plans not working out. I guess when yours did, I was upset." She also gave her the money back.

"I don't care about the money"

"No, you can keep it," Kimberly told her.

"It's my gift to you. I am rich, you know."

"Wow. You're still willing to give me the money after the way I treated you?"

"Hey, it's only money!" She smiled a warm smile at Rebecca.

"I guess I had you figured all wrong. You're not the person that I thought you to be."

"When most people get to know me, they feel the same way," Kimberly told her. Rebecca opened her computer and deleted all her files before Kimberly. She also gave her the original copy. She continued to apologize for her actions.

"Stop apologizing," Kimberly said.

"I tell you what; you can make it up to me by getting me a drink."

"What do you want?"

"I want vodka straight up. Fix yourself one, too, because you need to relax." Rebecca got up and fixed their drinks.

"Do you feel like taking a shower together?" Kimberly asked.

"Sure," Rebecca said.

"You go ahead and get in I'll be in there in a minute. Kimberly told her. I've got to get some things out of my car. Kimberly put her clothes on, went to the car, and got her bag. She came back inside. She put her bag slightly under the bed. After undressing, she got into the shower with Rebecca. She washed her body. They began kissing. Things were getting steamy. Kimberly and Rebecca got out of the shower. Rebecca went and sat in bed. Kimberly didn't. She walked around the opposite side of the bed and got her bag. While Rebecca wasn't watching, she pulled out the pistol and fired a shot at Rebecca. The bullet hit her in the back of the head, killing her. It was a one-shot kill. She then went to the other side of the bed where Rebecca's nude body lay and emptied the gun into her lifeless body.

"You stupid bitch! You should've known better than to fuck with me," she said as she shot her last bullet. She gathered everything that could link her to the crime. She took the sheets and put them in a large trash bag from her kitchen. She went into the bathroom and cleaned the shower. She put everything, including the gun, in a bag. She got the glass that she used. She then took Rebecca's laptop. She ransacked the place to make it look like a burglary. She went to her car and placed the bags in her back seat. She took the money that she had given Rebecca and left. Kimberly was filled with hatred for Rebecca, and she became enraged. She knew that she had to make her pay for her blackmail scheme.

The other reason she killed her was because she felt that her conscience would kick in, and she couldn't risk her revealing their scheme to Peyton or Gil. She left Rebecca's place, drove to a dumpster, and threw the bag in it. She then drove home and took another shower. She put her money back in the safe. She turned on her television and tried calling Peyton again. She was full of anxiety because Peyton wasn't answering her calls. She got her a drink and took a sedative to calm her nerves. She had resolved one of her problems; now all that was left to do was work on getting Peyton back. She had no idea that Peyton had no plans of going back. *"All I have to do is be patient,"* she thought. *"She'll be home soon. All I have to do is talk to her. Everything will be back to normal."* She went to sleep.

Chapter Fifteen

SUNDAY MORNING

Peyton woke early and went out on the deck to watch the sunrise. It is still a little dark out. The sounds of nature soothed her mind as she meditated, clearing her thoughts of all worries. Life was good for her. She had the anointing of peace over her life. Thirty minutes later, the sun came into full view, starting out bright orange and rising over the horizon. It brightened her mood as the beams bounced off the water and the lush lawn, showcasing a balance of colors that blended like a carefully painted masterpiece. Jan came out with a pot of coffee, bagels, cream cheese, and fresh fruit.

"What would you like for breakfast?" she asked Peyton.

"This is perfect. I don't want to eat a big breakfast. I'm going to church today, and I don't want to be sleepy during the service."

"Okay, well, if you change your mind, let me know." Jan left. Peyton continued to enjoy her morning outdoors. Jan came back about an hour later with the house phone.

"It's Mr. Wilkes, ma'am." Peyton took the phone. She was in a good mood. "Good morning," she said as she answered the phone.

"Well, good morning yourself. You sound upbeat this morning. How are you?" Gil said excitedly to hear her voice.

"I'm enjoying this beautiful morning that God has blessed me to see. It's so beautiful out here. I had almost forgotten how lovely and peaceful this place can be. That's why we initially bought the place. It's a shame we weren't out here more often." Peyton said while continuing to take in all the beauty. "God created this place with me in mind."

"Well do you think you can take a break a little later on and go to church with me?" he asked. She chuckled.

"I guess I can pull myself away."

"Great, I'll call you when I'm headed out." I'll see you soon," Gil said.

He went into his closet and got out one of his best suits. He chose one that Peyton picked out for him. His barber had come over the previous day to give him a haircut and a shave. He took his shower and when he was dressed, he looked at himself in the mirror. "Dang, that girl has got good taste," he said, referring to the suit that Peyton bought for him. He got his cell phone and called Peyton to let her know that he would be leaving. She got in her car. With nervous excitement, she drove down the driveway checking her makeup in the rearview mirror as she drove away.

When she arrived, Gil walked over and helped her out of her car. He looked much different than he had the last time she saw him. He was clean-shaven, and he looked handsome with his fresh haircut. *"He had to go all out,"* she thought. "Mmph!" she said as she looked at him. "You look fantastic." She couldn't take her eyes off him. He smiled at her as she stared at him. She hardly noticed that he had taken her hand to walk her into the church. She was falling in love with him all over again. She wanted to feel his arms around her once more. She gripped his hand tighter, and she wouldn't let go.

They walked into the sanctuary together. They sat in their usual seat. The other parishioners greeted them. Everyone they knew was excited to see Peyton. The service began, and the Word of God seemed spot-on for their situation. Pastor Hawkins spoke on restoration and reconciliation, which Gil was all for. After service, the pastor asked them to join him in his office for a brief meeting. They agreed. He spoke with them about the things the Lord had laid upon his heart. He also shared with them that he felt the Lord wanted them to work out their differences and return to him wholeheartedly. They listened with open minds. They didn't say much.

After the meeting, Gil walked her to her car. "Would you like to go eat?" he asked her. "I think I can do that," she replied. They went out. They ate and laughed and talked. They went back to the house where Peyton was staying. They saw no need to part ways because things between them were going so well. Once inside, they decided to watch movies. Gil got the television ready. When he turned on the television, the evening news was coming on. They saw a picture of Rebecca on the screen. The story of her death was out. She was the mayor's niece, and the detectives were asking the public for any information on who may have killed her. The news was shocking to them both. They couldn't believe what they were hearing. Peyton sat down with her hand over her mouth. "Oh my goodness! Who could've done such a thing?"

"I don't know," Gil said. They both sat there for a minute in disbelief. After the news, he put a movie on for Peyton. It was a romantic comedy of one of Peyton's favorite movies starring a famed Italian Hollywood actress named Delilah Castellucci. Peyton was grateful to him because she knew he preferred watching sports or action movies. Halfway through the show, she dozed off. Gil played with her hair as she slept. She had a heavenly glow. He whispered a prayer that if God would allow them to get back together, he would love and protect her. This is one of many prayers that he'd prayed over the past few months since their breakup. When Peyton woke, she apologized.

"I'm sorry," she said. I didn't mean to fall asleep on you."

"Oh, you're alright. You looked so peaceful. I was enjoying watching you." She sat up.

"How long was I asleep?"

"Not long," he said. She leaned into him, and he placed his arms around her. They continued to watch the movie; neither of them was really concentrating on it. They

237

enjoyed each other's company. Jan was getting ready to leave for the evening, so she wanted to see if they needed anything. They requested ice cream and apple pie.

"We are going to share," Peyton said, "Bring one saucer and two spoons."

"Bring coffee too." Jan went on to fill their request. Peyton looked at Gil and said,

"We still think alike."

"Well, of course we do. We're soulmates." Gil pulled her to him with a loving embrace and began kissing her. Peyton gave in to the kiss, and in the heat of passion, they hardly noticed when Jan entered the room. She gently placed the tray on the table and quietly backed away. They heard when she placed the tray on the coffee table. Gil said to Jan while still kissing his wife,

"That'll be all. We won't need anything else tonight." Jan took the queue and left for the evening. He and Peyton continued to enjoy each other. There was something spiritual yet sexy and passionate about their lovemaking. Husband and wife in the most beautiful session. It was spiritual and soulful. The very heavens were involved in their lovemaking God was smiling down upon them.

Something spectacular was taking place and they both knew it. All the trauma they experienced was eliminated. They were destined to be together for the rest of their lives. God miraculously healed their union. They recommitted their love to each other that day. They vowed never to separate again. Peyton was moving back into their home, leaving with Gil the following day. He canceled all appointments and spent the day with his wife.

They celebrated the evening with an extravagant dinner, then afterward they continued their festive night of fun and lovemaking. They were having more fun now, than ever. They made plans to take a trip and possibly renew their wedding vows. Gil went to work the following day. Peyton stayed home and got all her things back in order. Her cell phone rang. Thinking it was her husband, she answered without looking at the caller ID. It was Kimberly.

"Hey baby, did you forget something?" Kimberly was enraged but she kept her cool.

"Excuse me," Kimberly said.

"Oh Kimberly," she said surprised.

"How are you?"

"Who did you think that I was on the phone?" she asked.

"No one," Peyton said.

"So, what did this no one forget? I want to know. Is this no one taking my place in your life? Did you move out for this, no one?"

"Kimberly please calm down."

"What do you mean calm down? I've been calling you, but you've refused to answer my calls. They go straight to voicemail."

"Kimberly, I told you. I needed to take some time for myself." Not wanting to talk too long, Peyton said,

"Look I can't talk. I have to go."

"When can I see you?" Kimberly asked.

"Kimberly, I don't know if that would be a good idea."

"Look, baby, I'm not trying to put any pressure on you. I just want to see you. I want to make sure that you're okay. You know you went through so much when your husband cheated on you, and I know that you are still fragile, and I don't want you making any rash decisions, nor do I want anybody taking advantage of you."

By now, her eyes were opened, and she recognized her manipulation tactics. Peyton couldn't believe that she'd actually fallen for it before. She had been so full of heartbreak that she was too blind to see what was happening at the time. But it was plain to see. She wasn't falling for it. With this, she began to feel contempt and a sense of resentment, because Kimberly had manipulated her. She thought, "*I can't believe that I fell for that.*" As Kimberly continued her speech, Peyton interrupted her.

"Kimberly I'm okay. I'm doing well. I'm happy and I'm enjoying my life." Kimberly tried to continue.

"Kimberly I'm fine." Kimberly was frustrated. Peyton no longer wanted her, and she didn't need her in her life. She decided to go ahead and tell her everything. She expressed her feelings about their relationship.

"Kimberly, I moved back into my home with my husband. We're back together. We've decided to work on our marriage."

"I don't believe what I am hearing!" Kimberly shouted.

"After all that he's put you through and you took him back! What did he say to you to get you to come back to him? I'm telling you that he is taking advantage of you in your frail state."

"No!" Peyton said. "It was you who took advantage of our friendship to get me to sleep with you. You used my pain to lure me into your world. I loved you and I trusted you as my friend. We crossed the line. I was very uncomfortable living that lifestyle. I'm a married woman, and I'm also a Christian. It's time that I get my life together, and I suggest that you do the same. I love my husband. I always have. I want him and I want to work on our marriage. It was my decision, not Gil's. I made this choice on my own. He didn't manipulate me into anything. It was of my own free will."

Kimberly was crushed. She knew there was nothing she could say to change her mind. It was over and she knew it, but she wasn't going to let that be the end. Kimberly was growing increasingly unstable, and she wasn't thinking clearly. She had already killed Rebecca. The only thing keeping her from Peyton was Gil. She thought, "If I can get rid of Gil, she'll come back to me." Peyton broke her train of thought.

"I have to go Kimberly." Kimberly tried to be nice. "Okay, well it seems like you're happy. I'm happy for you. I promise not to interfere with your life. I didn't know that you still loved your husband. Trust me Peyton; I wasn't trying to trick you into loving me."

She went on with her sad story and pitiful apology. Peyton heard her out for a few more minutes and then she said to her,

"I'm glad that you understand. Now we both can move on with our lives." Peyton abruptly ended the call.

Kimberly was distraught without Peyton in her life and felt she had nothing left to live for. Their conversation showed that Peyton was no longer interested in a friendship, which upset her even more. She was delusional and in so much pain that she directed her anger toward Gil.

"He's got to go. He doesn't deserve her. She's mine. I love her, and I won't let anybody get in the way of us being together."

Her mind was officially gone. She went into her safe and got her pistol. She sat on her bed and looked at pictures of her and Peyton's trip to the Bahamas and Hawaii. She planned to go to their home and kill Gil there but it would be difficult due to all the security at their home. There was a large wrought iron gate at the Wilkes estate, and they had a six-man security team that consisted of several Memphis police officers. There was no way she would even make it onto the property. She couldn't just kill Gil right in Peyton's presence. She had to make it look like a random killing. She decided to get him while he was at his clinic. She knew his schedule. She felt this would be a better option. She began following and watching him over the next couple of days. In the meantime, Gil and Peyton were enjoying their lives. They went to her parent's home for dinner. Her parents were pleased to know they'd reconciled. They listened to the Brockington's stories of persevering in marriage. They shared a lot of pointers about their relationship, the good and the not-so-good times. They were sitting in the family room when the buzzer for the front gate rang. Gil jumped up and said, "I'll get it. I'm expecting a delivery." Peyton and her parents wondered who would be delivering at seven o'clock in the evening. Gil opened the remote gate, and he waited for his delivery. It took them about five minutes to come down to the Brockington's home. It was a florist. They brought in roses, and Gil took a single rose out and gave it to his wife. He had a ring case in his hands. He took her hand, got down on one knee, and proposed to her before her parents. She said yes. They continued to celebrate the evening. Peyton was overjoyed. She was ready to go home and enjoy her husband. As they left for home, unbeknownst to them, Kimberly was watching them. She sat outside the gate for almost an hour and went home.

Chapter Sixteen

DEADLY INTENT

Peyton and her mother were out shopping for wedding gowns for her vow renewal service. Her mother was overjoyed because Peyton had come back to her senses. She had been very concerned about her over the past few months because Kimberly had managed to isolate her from them, as well as anything or anyone familiar to her. This puzzled her parents because Peyton was a stable, well-rounded woman. Mrs. Brockington felt something wasn't quite right with Kimberly's possessive behavior. She was over-protective of Peyton in what seemed to be very dysfunctional, but she allowed her daughter to make her own choices without interference. They went into one of the most expensive and exclusive bridal boutiques in all of Memphis. It was difficult to get a booking. You had to know someone on the inside. Even the elite in the state found it difficult to book appointments. Somehow, Mrs. Brockington was able to book a fitting for her daughter.

"Wow, mom, these gowns are lovely," she said, looking through the gowns like an excited teenager looking for a prom dress.

"Yes, they're very beautiful," her mother replied. I happen to know the owner. She has a new line of exclusive gowns that I requested her to set aside just for you. Aside from a few others in the industry, you'll be given the first choice of your favorite gown."

"Wow, Mom! How'd you manage to swing that?"

"You and your father aren't the only ones with connections. I know a few people myself. That's how I was able to get this private showing. Hopefully, you can find what you like among these gowns. If not, I have a few more irons in the fire."

Peyton and her mother took their seats, along with a few other women. Wine and appetizers were provided while the live models walked the small runway in the featured gowns. After the showing, Peyton tried on several gowns. She narrowed her search down to two of her favorite gowns. She asked her mother to help her with the one she liked the most. Since her mother was a fashion designer, she could tell her where the dress needed alterations. While helping her daughter, she asked,

"How's Kimberly?"

"Oh, I guess she's okay."

"What's going on with her?"

"What do you mean, what's going on with her?" she asked while looking at the back of the gown she was trying on.

"I mean, what is she up to? How does she feel about you and Gil getting back together?"

"I don't know, I guess she's okay with it. Why?" Peyton wanted to know what her mom was getting at.

"Because I keep getting these bad vibes about her, and she's constantly on my mind, but not in a good way, ya know. It's like, something's not quite right with her. I can't put my finger on it but I'm feeling a bit disturbed in my spirit."

"Well, you don't have to worry about her. I had a talk with her. I told her that Gil and I are back together."

"And?"

"And that was that. She didn't like it at first, but she knew it was my choice."

"Why wouldn't she like the thought of you two getting back together?"

"I guess she felt Gil wasn't good enough for me because of what happened between us. Mom, can we not talk about her right now? I'm in a great mood and I don't want to think about any of that. Come and help me out of this dress."

"Okay. I'll leave it alone, but I'm getting some strange vibes. I know she's your friend, and I know you two are very close, but just for my sake, can you please not have anything to do with her for now?" her mom said with worry in her eyes. Peyton knew that her mother must've been on to something so she promised her that she would stay away from Kimberly. Peyton had no intention of going around her anyway and this latest warning from her mother was only confirmation of what she was already feeling inside. Peyton couldn't choose between the two gowns, so she reserved them both, and they continued shopping.

Peyton called Gil. He told her that he would be working well into the night and if she wanted, she could come down to the clinic. They would be taking a much-needed vacation after their vow renewal. She agreed to stop by and bring dinner with her. After she and her mom were done shopping for the day, Peyton went home with her mom and stayed there until time for her to go to the clinic with Gil. She hung out with her father and watched television with him. He was feeling much better, and the doctor said that he would be able to return to the firm in a couple of months. As long as he took it easy and took care of himself, he was going to be just fine. Mrs. Brockington came in with dinner for Mr. Brockington.

"Peyton, would you like me to fix something for you?"

"No, Mom. Gil and I are going to eat together."

"That reminds me; I have to get going." Peyton got her purse, kissed her dad, and hugged her mother.

"I'll see you guys tomorrow. I'll be here to pick you up so that we can find some shoes to go with my gown."

"Okay darling. Be careful. I love you."

"Love you too, Mom. I love you Dad"

Instead of getting something to eat, she headed over to the clinic. She was going to have something delivered. It was around six-thirty when she made it. A couple of the girls were just leaving. They spoke to her as they were exiting the building. She went inside where Gil was. He was in his office. She was happy to see him. He was overlooking patient files.

"Where do these go?" she asked looking at a pile of patient folders that he had stacked on the floor.

"I'll get the girls to file those away tomorrow. They've already been entered into the system. They're the last of the patients that I have follow-up care with. I'm releasing them next week. After that, it's some much-needed time off for me. I'm ready to spend some time with my beautiful wife."

"You've got that right baby," Peyton said as she leaned over him and kissed him. Peyton got her cell phone and looked for a nice restaurant for delivery.

"What do you want for dinner?" she asked.

"You," he replied. She laughed.

"That'll be your dessert. Now, what do you want for dinner?"

"I don't know, maybe something from that Italian restaurant that you like so much."

"Would you like your favorite?"

"Yes," he said. Peyton ordered dinner for them and requested that it be delivered to the clinic. The phone rang at the clinic.

"I wonder who could be calling at this time," he thought. He answered but the caller hung up on him. After about thirty minutes the back doorbell rang.

"That'll be the food," he said. He placed the files on his desk and ran down the back hallway to get the food. While he was doing that, the phone to the clinic rang again. Peyton answered. It was the Italian restaurant calling to confirm their order and the time that they would be there to deliver. Peyton was wondering who could be at the back door. She thought that it was probably one of the employees and perhaps they had left something until she heard Gil say out loud,

"Kimberly, you don't have to do this!" Peyton ran down the back hall to see what was happening. When she got there, Kimberly was standing in the doorway with a gun pointed at Gil. Peyton was frightened.

"Kimberly, what are you doing?" she asked.

"I'm here to get what rightfully belongs to me," she said.

"I love you, Peyton, and this man doesn't deserve to live for all the things that he put you through. He has harmed you, and now he has brainwashed you into coming back to him. I will not stand for that. I will stop at nothing to get you back! Rebecca tried to get in my way, and I had to take care of her. Now all that's left is to take care of this traitor." Peyton was frightened.

"So, it was you who killed Rebecca?"

"You're damn right I killed that whore. She didn't deserve to live for all the hell that she put me through, and neither does this motherfucker right here."

Kimberly was so focused on Peyton, that she didn't notice Gil had grabbed her wrist and twisted it. They began to struggle over the gun. They both fell to the floor. A shot rang out, and Peyton stood still, horrified about the events unfolding before her. She didn't know who had been shot. Gil sprang to his feet. Kimberly grabbed his leg. He tried to fight her off. He fired another shot into her body. She stopped moving. Peyton was screaming and shaking uncontrollably. She was in shock by what she had just witnessed. Gil put his arm around her trying to get her to calm down. He called the police. The whole thing was caught on security cameras. It was a justifiable homicide. Gil was cleared by the police department. They also told the police that Kimberly had confessed to them that she had killed Rebecca.

WEDDING DAY

Peyton was awakened to breakfast in bed from Gil, who was standing over her with a tray full of bacon and eggs, pancakes, fresh fruit, coffee, and a dozen orange roses. She looked up at him and smiled. "Your breakfast, ma'am," he said. She sat up in bed, and he placed the tray on her lap, giving her a warm kiss in the process.

"Thank you, darling," she said kissing him back.

"I'm going to need some help eating this or I won't be able to fit into my gown today."

"I don't think that's going to be a problem."

"You're just being kind," she said. Gil had the cook make enough for them both so that they could eat breakfast in their room. After they finished eating, they held each other.

"Are you nervous?" Gil asked.

"No, not really. How about you?"

"I'm excited and I can't believe it's happening for us. Just a couple of months ago I had just about lost all hope that there would be any chance of us even talking, let alone getting remarried. I'm truly grateful to our Heavenly Father for sending you back to me.

During your absence, I learned a lot of things about myself. I felt my life was over without you in it. I began to see myself in a whole new light. I saw my shortcomings in our relationship. I realized how selfish I had been. I could've been a better husband to you. It was like I had to re-evaluate who I was as a person and a husband. I made a promise to God that if He ever allowed us to have a second chance, I would do things much differently and I would strive to be the best husband possible. You've been nothing but good to me in our marriage. You've always loved me and put me and my needs ahead of your own. You're a woman of integrity and I know that I can always trust you."

At that point, Peyton felt a little guilty about her former relationship with Kimberly. She needed to tell Gil the whole truth about her and Kimberly before they renewed their vows. That way, there would be no secrets between them, and nothing would come up later to cause them any more problems.

"Gil," she said hoping to lay it all out in the open.

"I don't want there to be any secrets between us and I want you to know everything about me and Kimberly." Gil placed his finger over her lips and said, "Shhh! You don't have to go into that. Anything that you did while we were apart is between you and God. As the bible says. *"If any man is in Christ, he's a new person. Old things have gone away, and all things are new."* We're now a new couple in Christ, and that's all that matters. Anything you thought you wanted to tell me; I don't need to know because it is all under the Blood of Jesus. I love you Peyton." He gently lifted her chin and kissed her softly on the lips. Her heart melted, and she willingly gave in to the kiss, and they held each other with all their might. They were interrupted by the phone ringing. It was Peyton's mother.

"Are you two ready for today?" Peyton could hear the joy in her mother's voice.

"We're finishing breakfast, Mom; we will be ready soon."

"Your father and I will be on our way around twelve-thirty."

"That'll be fine mom, I'll see you then."

The wedding was taking place at their home. All the guests seemed to arrive at the same time. The caterer, the stylists, and the photographers were at the door. The intercom was constantly buzzing in their bedroom. Peyton ran downstairs to greet everyone and to point them to their respective places. Their chef, Mrs. Silvia demanded that Peyton go and get dressed and allow her to do her job. She took care of everything while Peyton was getting ready for her big day. She went upstairs and put on her wedding gown. Her mother knocked on her bedroom door and let herself in. She helped her with her gown and accessories. "You look lovely darling," her mother said.

"Thank you Mom."

"I'm so happy for you two. I know it's been a rough couple of months for both of you, but there are times when couples tend to go through rough patches. In the end, it makes for a stronger union. When you're able to endure the tough times, it seems to seal your bond."

"Mom, I love you, and I want to thank you for always being here for me and for allowing me to make my own decisions. I want you to know that I value your insight. I thank God for you and Daddy." Her mother embraced her tightly.

"I know; now let's get you down to this man. He's so nervous that he's shaking in those pricey new shoes of his. He acts like it's his first time down the aisle."

They both laughed. As she made her way down the grand marble staircase, she noticed her father standing at the edge of the stairs waiting to walk her outside and down the aisle. He took her by the arm, kissed her on the cheek, and said, "You're still the most beautiful girl in the world, baby girl." He walked her outdoors, and they began their journey down the aisle. The guest list included close family and friends. Time stood still as Peyton floated down the aisle towards him. Feeling like God had shown him favor once again, he happily took her by the hand and they both faced the minister. He couldn't take his eyes off her. He whispered, "You're stunning!" She mouthed the words,

"Thank you." She smiled, trying to focus on what Pastor Hawkins was saying. After the ceremony was over, they were presented to their guests. They enjoyed their guests and partied most of the day. The following morning, they were off on their second honeymoon, this time to

Paris. They were on their flight getting settled in. Gil leaned into his wife for a kiss.

"You know, I'm the luckiest man alive. God has blessed me with a wonderful career, prosperity, and peace, and I can truly say that I have been shown favor because He's allowed me to marry the most beautiful woman in the world not once but twice. I must've done something right in my past life."

She was overjoyed; all she could do was smile.

"I have a present for you," she said. She reached into her bag and took out a gift box. He opened it and saw a pair of baby shoes. He looked at them puzzled.

"Do you like them?" she asked.

"Peyton, are you telling me…?"

"Yes, I'm telling you that you're going to be a father."

Tears began to flow down his cheeks. He gently held his wife; "I'm going to be a father!" By now, tears were flowing from her eyes seeing his reaction.

"I love you Gil"

"I love you too."

They embraced.

CONCLUSION

No matter your situation or your circumstances, you can always find your way back home to your Heavenly Father. He's always there to watch over you and to lead and guide you into His peace. Our fictional sister and dear friend Peyton was caught up in a relationship that did not agree with her inner spirit. You, too, may find yourself in relationships that are not in agreement with your inner spirit. It doesn't have to be like the one Peyton found herself in. It could be anything that grieves your spirit and stunts your growth, hindering you from reaching your God-given potential or destiny. Our friend Peyton didn't know how she would get out of her situation, but when she called on her Father, He came to her and comforted her. He forgave her, helped her out of her predicament, and set her on a path toward her destiny.

Although the story is fiction, some people find themselves trapped in things they believe will bring them comfort and peace, which ultimately brings turmoil and pain. I, too, have found myself in toxic friendships, relationships, predicaments, and negative situations that I thought would bring comfort, only to find pain and destruction. With the Father's help, I found my way back on the path towards my destiny.

Not only does He put you back on the right path for your life, but He also blesses your life.

God is Truly Awesome!!!!!

I'd like to thank you personally for your time reading the book "Closer than Enemies" I hope you enjoyed the journey. I pray the Blessings and Peace of our Heavenly Father be upon your life,

Karen

ABOUT THE AUTHOR

Karen Coleman is an Arkansas native. She enjoys writing exciting and dramatic stories. A phenomenal author with a distinctive style, she has demonstrated a sensational talent for steering her readers through every line and page with eager anticipation.

Karen has published several novels in various genres. Readers have described her novels as riveting, fast-paced, and thrilling.
Her teen novels are insightful and empowering. As a mentor who has worked with teens for many years, Karen understands the social challenges they face, and she skillfully addresses those topics with a finesse that lends excitement, adventure, and encouragement.

A self-proclaimed writer of fiction with an element of truth, Karen began penning her thoughts as a hobby. After many years of writing and encouragement from those around her, she began writing on a more intense level, eventually turning out several wonderful novels. She offers something for almost every reader, from her adult crime series to her teen books, there's something to be enjoyed by all. Her literary works have garnered much fanfare and have not only been enjoyed by her many readers; she's highly celebrated among her writing peers. Her books are meant to inspire, uplift, and entertain leaving her audience asking for more.

Karen is also a playwright, actor, and former city council member. She's the mother of four and a Glam-ma of thirteen and counting. Her grandchildren affectionately call her Nana. She's also the proud mom of two rambunctious miniature schnauzers. When not writing or spoiling her grandbabies, she spends her time crafting, fishing, or enjoying a great barbecue.

Other Books by the Author

Arkansas Heat "A City Scorned"
Arkansas Heat "A Brutha's Obsession"
Arkansas Heat "Cindy's Revenge"
Arkansas Heat "Raising Delgado"
Arkansas Heat "Deceptive Practice"
Closer Than Enemies 1
Closer Than Enemies 2
Frozen Dreams
In the Wrong Game
No Place for Emily Ann
Metamorphosis "Good Girl Gone Bad"
Morgan's Path
Whatever Happened to I love you?

Be on the lookout for several more exciting projects.

Also check out the audio versions on Amazon, Audible.com, and iTunes

www.ingramcontent.com/pod-product-compliance
Lightning Source LLC
Chambersburg PA
CBHW020746250626
47155CB00003B/939